SECRETS OF THE
CASTLETON
MANOR LIBRARY™

Page Fright

Elizabeth Penney

Annie's®
AnniesFiction.com

Books in the Secrets of the Castleton Manor Library series

A Novel Murder
Bitter Words
The Grim Reader
A Deadly Chapter
An Autographed Mystery
Second Edition Death
A Crime Well Versed
A Murder Unscripted
Pride and Publishing
A Literary Offense
Up to Noir Good
For Letter or Worse
On Pens and Needles
Ink or Swim
Tell No Tales
Page Fright
A Fatal Yarn
Read Between the Crimes
From Fable to Grave
A Fateful Sentence
Cloak and Grammar
A Lost Clause
A Thorny Plot
A Scary Tale Wedding

Page Fright
Copyright © 2018, 2021 Annie's.

All rights reserved. No part of this publication may be reproduced, stored in a retrieval system, or transmitted in any form or by any means—electronic, mechanical, photocopying, recording or otherwise—without the prior written permission of the publisher. The only exception is brief quotations in printed reviews. For information address Annie's, 306 East Parr Road, Berne, Indiana 46711-1138.

The characters and events in this book are fictional, and any resemblance to actual persons or events is coincidental.

Library of Congress-in-Publication Data
Page Fright / by Elizabeth Penney
p. cm.
I. Title
2018945958

AnniesFiction.com
(800) 282-6643
Secrets of the Castleton Manor Library™
Series Creator: Shari Lohner
Series Editor: Lorie Jones
Cover Illustrator: Jesse Reisch

10 11 12 13 14 | Printed in China | 9 8 7 6 5 4

1

The first rocket hissed into the night sky, exploding into showers of brilliant colors reflected in the bay below.

Faith Newberry and a group of spectators huddled on Castleton Manor's cliffs. They oohed and aahed, their upturned faces catching the light. Before the first sparks fully died, another rocket shot off and burst into glorious display.

"I'm freezing." Brooke Milner shivered and moved closer to Faith. "But I don't want to go inside and miss anything."

Faith tugged the wool hat knit by her aunt Eileen farther down over her ears. "I'm a block of ice myself. But you have to admit this is a great way to celebrate New Year's Eve." She pointed to the bonfire, where hot drinks and baked goods were being dispensed. "Let's go warm up and get another cup of cocoa."

With Faith's tuxedo cat, Watson, at their heels, the two women edged their way through the crowd.

Faith and Brooke worked at Castleton Manor in Lighthouse Bay, Massachusetts, where book retreats and other literary events were held. Faith was the librarian, and Brooke was the head chef.

Tonight's gathering was the inaugural event for Everything Shakespeare, a ten-day celebration in honor of the Bard. A theater troupe would be rehearsing and then performing condensed versions of William Shakespeare's plays in the manor.

This retreat had a slightly different format than most that were held at Castleton, which were mainly restricted to guests, with occasional public events. For Everything Shakespeare, only the theater troupe was staying at the manor. Tickets for the plays were being sold to the public, accompanied by a robust advertising campaign aimed as far away as Boston.

As they approached the refreshment booth, Brooke elbowed Faith. "I'm glad Wolfe made it back from London in time to see the fireworks."

Faith's heart gave a little hop when she saw Wolfe Jaxon. The tall, handsome businessman stood near the fire, deep in conversation with his mother, Charlotte Jaxon, and a middle-aged man. Tonight Wolfe wore a long wool overcoat and a cashmere muffler against the chill.

"He told me last week that he would be here," Faith said, trying to sound casual. Brooke was always trying to read romance into Faith's friendship with Wolfe. "This event is important to Charlotte. Her good friend Bates Beaumont is directing the plays."

"That's probably him." In the flickering firelight, Brooke narrowed her eyes as she studied the man. "He's not bad-looking. I wonder if he's interested in Charlotte." Wolfe's father had died years before.

Faith sighed at Brooke's relentless matchmaking, but she had to agree with her assessment. Whoever he was, he had a full head of gray hair and craggy but attractive features.

Meanwhile, Watson had padded ahead, eager to warm his black-and-white fur by the fire.

Wolfe smiled when he saw the bobtailed cat, and he bent to stroke Watson's chin. Then he glanced around, obviously seeking Watson's owner. When he spotted Faith, his smile broadened.

"Let's go say hello," Brooke said, taking Faith's arm.

Not reluctant in the least, Faith allowed herself to be tugged along.

"Happy New Year, ladies," Wolfe said when they reached his side. "Enjoying the party?"

"We sure are." Faith glanced upward, where fireworks continued to decorate the sky, then around at the ever-growing crowd. "It seems like half of Lighthouse Bay is here tonight."

Unfortunately, her aunt Eileen, head librarian at the Candle House Library, was recovering from a cold so she had stayed home. Faith's other good friend, concierge veterinarian Midge Foster, was on a ski trip with her family. Midge also ran the pet bakery Happy Tails in town.

"I'm glad we received such a good response to our invitation," Charlotte said. Like her son, she was tall and trim and had elegant, patrician features. "I hope they all come back for the plays too."

"Don't worry," the man standing next to Charlotte said, his voice a pleasant rumble. "Our cast of actors always packs the house." He thrust out a hand to Faith. "Hi. I'm Bates Beaumont."

Faith introduced herself and Brooke and explained their roles at the manor.

"I'm very happy to meet you both," Bates said, giving a slight bow. "The library is fabulous, and I've heard the food is also." He patted his slight paunch. "Not that I need to indulge."

A lanky young woman in her early twenties appeared behind Bates, slinking around to take his arm and lean against him. She had flowing red hair and oddly pale blue eyes. "Hello, Papa. What's going on?" Her petulant gaze flickered over Faith and Brooke.

Bates drew her forward. "Perdita, dear, come meet some of Castleton's excellent staff."

Perdita? Faith didn't think she'd ever heard the unusual name outside Shakespeare's *The Winter's Tale*. She joined Brooke in greeting the newcomer.

"Wolfe and Charlotte," Bates said, "I've been meaning to tell you something. And now that we're in the company of the charming Miss Newberry, it's the ideal time."

"Don't tell me," Charlotte said. "Not the—"

Bates nodded. "I brought my *First Folio* with me. I thought it could be displayed during our performances. In a locked case, of course."

"Of course," Faith echoed faintly, trying to hide her shock.

The Shakespeare *First Folio* was one of the world's literary treasures. The bound volume of plays was valued in the millions. She couldn't believe that Bates had traveled with such a valuable book.

Perdita folded her arms across her chest and scowled. "I told you not to bring it." Her eyes glinted. "It's going to be mine someday, and I'm rather partial to the thing."

Her father waved a hand. "I'm not dead yet, so I make the decisions."

"It's not sitting in your room, is it?" Wolfe asked. "Not that our staff isn't trustworthy, but something worth millions is very tempting."

Perdita gasped. "What were you thinking?" She began to hammer on her father's shoulder with her fists.

Watson, who'd been seated nearby, squawked and scampered away.

Bates dodged his daughter's blows, finally grabbing her wrists to make her stop. "The *First Folio* is perfectly secure." He laughed heartily, seeming unperturbed by Perdita's anger. "It's locked in the manor's safe."

Perdita glowered at him.

"Let's go watch the fireworks closer to the water." Bates threaded his arm through his daughter's and tugged her away.

As they wandered off, snatches of their squabble drifted back to the little group.

"Oh my," Brooke whispered, low enough that only Faith heard her remark.

"I do enjoy Perdita," Charlotte said. "But I rather wish she'd stayed home. With her issues . . ."

Wolfe sent Faith and Brooke a look of alarm. "Mother, that's not very discreet of you." With a resolute sigh, he said to his employees, "Since you unfortunately witnessed that display, may I ask you to please keep an eye on Perdita this week? She's only recently gotten out of the hospital."

Faith unfortunately could guess the type of facility it had been. "Of course we will." Inwardly she hoped the volatile young woman didn't complicate an already jam-packed schedule.

"If there are any problems," his mother added, "please let me or Wolfe know immediately."

Wolfe turned to Faith. "I appreciate your assisting the stage manager during the event, so I've asked Laura to help you out this week."

College student Laura Kettrick was a housekeeper at the manor, and she occasionally assisted Faith in the library.

"And due to the intensity of the performance schedule," Wolfe continued, "I'd like all three of you to stay on-site. We've assigned you a suite."

Brooke gave a hoot, then clapped a hand over her mouth, blushing. "Sorry. It's just that I've always wanted to stay at the manor. I thought it would help me understand the guest experience."

"Which is excellent, thanks to your culinary skills, Brooke." Charlotte smiled. "I hope you ladies enjoy yourselves in the William Shakespeare Suite."

"That is so kind of you," Faith said, trying to suppress her own excitement. The elegant rooms in the suite were decorated in medieval style, with tapestries, canopy beds, and plush velvet furniture. Queen Elizabeth I would have felt very much at home.

"Oh, and be sure to bring Watson along," Charlotte said. "I've had a special pet bed put in there for him to sleep in." She grinned. "It has a canopy."

Faith was almost overcome by Charlotte's thoughtfulness, but before she could thank her, a series of rockets launched into the sky, accompanied by booms.

"It's the grand finale," Wolfe said, raising his voice to be heard. "Let's watch."

The group faced the water, where a dozen fireworks lit up the sky, exploding one after another.

Faith allowed herself to be swept up into the moment, watching the spectacle between two of her favorite people, Brooke and Wolfe.

Then something solid and furry pressed against her ankles. She scooped up her beloved cat, who snuggled close and purred.

"You're one of my favorites too, Watson," she whispered into his fur.

His fervent rub against her cheek assured her that he had assumed as much.

After the last spark died in the sky, the observers began making their way through the gardens back to the manor. There a late supper was to be served, with music and games as the last day of the year drew to a close. A special surprise had been planned to precede the stroke of midnight.

When they reached the tiled terrace, Brooke excused herself and headed for the kitchen to supervise the meal.

Faith entered the Great Hall Gallery with the other guests, stunned at the transformation wrought while they had been enjoying the fireworks.

The long, marble-floored hall was lit by tall electric candelabras that illuminated the thick tapestries and hangings on the walls. The second-floor balconies and archways had been twined with garland and twinkling lights. Along the walls, small tables had been set up for people to enjoy food and drink dispensed by costumed servers. Pots of rosemary and bowls of nuts and oranges decorated the tables.

Bates came up alongside Faith and took her arm, startling her. "Is this a good time to show you the *Folio*?"

Faith glanced around to see what was going on.

Standing near the statue of Agatha Christie, Charlotte greeted the guests with a very modern microphone. "First up is a game of Shakespeare charades," she announced. "We'll play in teams."

The *First Folio* was much more interesting than charades, so she said to Bates, "This is as good a time as any. Would you like to meet me in the library?"

Bates nodded. "Done. See you in a few." He turned and strode down the hall toward the lobby.

With Watson at her heels, Faith walked to the library and unlocked the door. To her delight, she saw that one of the staff members had lit the fire in the massive carved wood fireplace. Watson headed for the red velvet settee near the hearth while Faith slipped off her coat and hung it on the back of her desk chair.

Through the thick wooden door, the merriment of the crowd was muffled. She moved closer to the fire's warmth, allowing the library's quiet peace to seep in. In addition to the fragrance of burning applewood, the room held her favorite aromas—old paper, leather, and wood. Even if blindfolded, she would know that she was in a library, the most heavenly of rooms.

A rapping sounded on the door.

"Come in," she called.

The door swung open. Carrying a leather satchel, Bates entered, followed by Wolfe.

The director's gaze fell on Watson curled up in front of the fire. "That cat has the best seat in the house."

In response, Watson stretched, yawned, and curled into an even tighter ball.

"That's his favorite spot, especially in the winter," Faith said.

"It would be mine too." Bates tipped his head and studied the towering lines of books. "What a fantastic library." He clapped Wolfe on the shoulder. "It's so good of your family to share."

"It would be rather selfish to keep it all to ourselves," Wolfe replied. He indicated the satchel. "And I could say the same for you."

Bates smiled modestly. "Where shall I set my treasure, Miss Newberry?"

"Over here is fine." Faith directed him to a long table, then opened her desk drawer and pulled out three pairs of white gloves. They needed to wear them if they handled the rare, fragile book, printed almost four hundred years ago. Such antiquity boggled the mind.

Bates unzipped the satchel and removed a gray archival box, which he unfastened to reveal the volume, bound in faded brown leather.

The three of them stared at the book in silence for a long moment.

Then Bates slid on a glove and carefully opened the cover. The familiar face of the Bard gazed out from the title page.

"'Mr. William Shakespeare's Comedies, Histories, and Tragedies,'" Bates whispered, quoting the text. "Isn't it magnificent?"

"It is indeed," Wolfe said. He'd inherited the Jaxon love of books so evident in Castleton Manor's library, which held thousands of titles. "How wonderful that centuries later, we are still enjoying this man's work."

"It's an honor and a privilege to direct his plays," Bates said. "No one quite understands the human condition like William Shakespeare. Love, death, madness—"

Something creaked in the stacks on the second floor, which was open to the main room of the library.

All of them looked up, even Watson.

"Must be the wind," Faith said. "It's really picking up."

"The weather report said a snowstorm is on the way." Wolfe glanced toward the French doors, which opened onto a front terrace. "And there are the first flakes. An hour earlier and we would have had to cancel the fireworks."

"I'm glad we didn't have to," Faith murmured. "They were spectacular."

As Bates continued to gently turn the pages, Faith noted the vivid print on the ancient paper. "What quality," she remarked. "I somehow doubt many contemporary books will look this good in four hundred years."

"It's the rag paper," Bates said, running a finger down the page. "It absorbs the ink well and is highly resistant to deterioration."

On the balcony, the door to the upstairs hallway opened, revealing a rectangle of light and two figures.

"This is a shortcut to the Great Hall Gallery," a male voice said. "Go down those stairs and through the library, and you'll be right there."

"Thank you, kind squire," a woman said with a giggle. "Will you escort me? I'll have trouble on the spiral stairs with these skirts."

The woman had a slight accent Faith couldn't define. She thought she detected a touch of Italian.

"Of course, milady." The man bowed.

Wolfe shook his head. "I thought that door was locked."

Faith shifted from foot to foot in discomfort. Securing the library was her responsibility. "It should have been. I'm sorry, but I don't know what happened. I always make sure both doors are locked before leaving."

The trio watched in silence as the young couple strolled along the balcony toward the spiral staircase. The woman wore a medieval costume, complete with wimple and veils, and the man was dressed in the Castleton staff outfit of a white shirt and black pants.

Faith didn't know the woman, but she recognized Shaw Hastings. She'd seen him around the manor during the past few days. He was a new employee, and that was probably why he didn't realize that he shouldn't let people into the library after hours without her permission.

Wolfe appeared tense, and Faith could tell he was boiling. But she knew that he wouldn't reprimand a staff person in front of anyone else. He was first and foremost a gentleman.

Bates, gloved hand still resting on the *First Folio*, frowned. "That's Viola Grey, our leading lady."

The library door swung open. A man dressed in a doublet, tights, and a huge pancake hat stood there in a wide-legged stance, one hand resting dramatically on the dagger he wore. Faith hoped it was only a prop.

The man scanned the room. "Where is she?"

"Griffith, what's going on?" Bates asked. His tone was firm but kind.

Griffith ignored the director as he moved farther into the library. His restless gaze finally landed upon the couple inching their way down the spiral staircase. With an exclamation, he bolted across the room, his soft pointed shoes whispering on the carpet.

"Is this part of a performance?" Faith asked the others.

Wolfe shrugged.

His brow creased in concern, Bates didn't respond as he continued to watch Griffith.

Griffith halted below the balcony and drew his dagger. "Unhand her, you varlet."

Viola laughed. "Griffith, what on earth are you doing?" She paused on the step, one hand gripping the banister, the other, her companion's arm. "He's only helping me down the stairs."

Griffith strode closer, squinting up at the couple. He visibly deflated when they moved out of the shadows. "Oh. I thought you were with Corin. Someone said—"

Viola turned to Shaw. "What's your name?"

"Shaw Hastings."

"Griffith Andrews, meet Shaw Hastings," Viola said. "He works here."

Griffith straightened with a lurch, throwing his shoulders back. His voice dripped with animosity when he said, "Shaw Hastings? I never thought I'd see you here of all places."

2

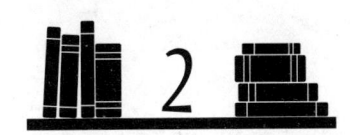

Faith tensed, certain that the two men were going to start fighting. *How did Griffith know Shaw, and what had Shaw done to warrant such hostility?*

"Oh boy. Griffith has his dander up." Bates sighed. "Not a good thing."

"I'll take care of it." Wolfe marched toward the stairs, his stride radiating authority.

Seeing his boss approaching, Shaw dropped Viola's hand and began to back up the staircase. "I think you're all set now, miss. Good luck with your performance." A moment later, the upper door banged shut.

"Good work scaring him away," Viola told Griffith. She reached out a hand to him. "You'd better come help me down."

Griffith climbed the narrow stairs two at a time. He took her hand and guided her down slowly.

"Hold on," Wolfe said. "What is going on here?"

Viola leaned forward, her large brown eyes widening. Under the ridiculous wimple, her heart-shaped face was delicate. "Who are you? A rescuer of damsels in distress, by chance?"

"I'm Wolfe Jaxon, co-owner of the manor." Resting his hands on his hips, he fixed both actors with a level stare. "While I'm very glad to have you all here this week, I must ask that you behave with decorum. There will be no duels or altercations in the library. Or anywhere else on the grounds for that—"

The haunting melody of "Greensleeves" echoed through the room.

Bates patted his pocket and pulled out a cell phone. "Please excuse me. I must take this." The terseness of his tone caused the others to wait silently during the call. A moment later he disconnected. "I have bad news. We're down an actor. Will is in the hospital with pneumonia."

Griffith's forehead furrowed. "How will we find another actor this close to opening night?" He glanced down, obviously realizing he was still holding the dagger, and sheathed it in one lithe move.

Bates pressed his lips together. "I suppose I can try the agencies in Boston and New York. When they open after the holiday." Due to the timing of New Year's Eve, that would be at least a few days from now. It was time the troupe didn't have.

Viola gave a little squeal. "I have an idea." She pointed at Wolfe. "You should fill in. You'd be perfect to take Will's place."

To Faith's surprise, Wolfe didn't immediately refuse. Although caught cold, he appeared to consider the proposal.

"I wouldn't have much time to learn the parts," Wolfe finally said. He tapped his temple. "I've got a pretty good memory, but two days of rehearsal would be pushing it."

"Will had very few lines," Bates said. "He was the third man, filling in the blanks for our stars, who carry the dialogue."

"We could cut the script even more," Viola suggested. "These are condensed plays already."

"I'll be all right," Wolfe said. He glanced at Faith. "Perhaps with a little coaching from our assistant stage manager."

A wave of heat flashed over Faith at the suggestion that she work closely with Wolfe on his lines. "I'll be happy to do that." She knew that if Brooke were here, she'd be rubbing her hands with glee.

Griffith held up a finger. "With all due respect, I need to ask." He winced as though aware the question might insult his host. "Do you have any stage experience?"

"I do." Wolfe chuckled. "It's been a couple of decades, but I acted in a few amateur Shakespeare productions when I was in college. We gave the proceeds to a local charity. I'm sure I still remember something from those days."

Somehow the idea of a young Wolfe working to help a charity in his free time didn't surprise Faith at all.

"That will suffice, I'm sure," Bates said. He slid his phone into his pocket. "Any port in a storm, right?"

"Speaking of which, look at that." Viola motioned to the French doors, where the wind was flinging snow against the glass. "It's a blizzard out there."

The library door opened yet again, and the sound of recorders and lutes drifted inside.

A woman with brown hair rushed in. "It's almost curtain time, folks."

Faith recognized Audrey Crowe, the stage manager she would be assisting.

"I'll be right there," Viola called. In her haste to leave, she promptly tripped on her hem.

Griffith rushed over and caught her before she fell.

Bates bustled toward the table, where the *First Folio* still sat. "Let's put this in a safe place."

"How about in this case?" Wolfe asked. He pulled out a set of keys and unlocked a softly lit glass cabinet. "Faith and I have the only sets of keys."

"That will do. Thank you." Bates carefully placed the rare book on the glass shelf and gave it a loving pat of farewell. "I'd better get out there and make sure everything is under control."

The actors whirled past them into the Great Hall Gallery, followed by Bates, who moved at a more sedate pace.

After checking that the second-floor door was indeed locked this time, Faith and Wolfe prepared to leave the library themselves.

"I'll come get you after the performance," Faith told Watson, who barely budged in response.

The Great Hall Gallery was now filled with medieval music, and as Faith walked into the main area, trumpets sounded. This must be the surprise event.

A small group of madrigal singers dressed in costume emerged onto a balcony above. She noticed Viola and Griffith among them.

Bates stepped up to the microphone. After greeting the audience, he said, "Music was a vital part of Elizabethan life, much as it is today. Of course, there weren't Top 40 hits or digital downloads."

The crowd laughed.

"But Shakespeare's plays are full of songs," Bates continued. "Tonight we will perform a few for you, and hopefully it will whet your appetite for our roster of plays."

The madrigal singers burst into the first piece, the male and female voices blending in perfect harmony.

Faith found a printed program on a nearby table and saw that the piece was called "Heart's Ease" from *Romeo and Juliet*.

Movement in the balcony across from the performers caught her eye. Perdita was standing near the rail watching, a veil over her flowing hair. Next to her was Shaw. He wore a jester's hat, like the rest of the Castleton servers.

She turned her attention back to the singers, noticing that Viola was in the front row. A man with curly dark hair stood next to her. He had narrow yet attractive features that reminded her of a fox. Faith assumed he was the actor Corin Huntington.

Griffith stood in the second row. He frequently glanced between Viola and Corin with a subtle frown. Audrey was beside him, singing with gusto, but her gaze was fixed on Griffith.

Intrigue among the players, Faith noted with amusement.

The door to the terrace cracked open, and a slight figure entered. The person pushed back a red hood, and Faith recognized Laura. Smoothing her fine, flyaway blonde hair into place, Laura scanned the crowd. Spotting Faith, she smiled and edged her way through the spectators.

"Sorry I'm late," Laura whispered in Faith's ear. She slipped off her coat and placed it on a chair, then returned to Faith's side. Her mouth dropped open at the sight of the costumed singers on the decorated balcony. "Wow."

"I feel like we've been transported back to Shakespeare's time," Faith said in an undertone. "Isn't it gorgeous?"

Laura nodded as she studied the performers. "I know some of these people." She gave Shaw a little wave. She'd helped him get the job at Castleton.

The performers concluded the song to great applause and then started a second number, this one a lively, foot-stomping tune. To the group's delight, several couples began to dance, weaving back and forth in intricate movements.

"Was that planned?" Laura asked.

"I don't think so," Faith said. "Judging by the look on Marlene's face."

Marlene Russell watched from the sidelines, wearing her trademark sour expression. The assistant manager hated it when people deviated from the established routine. But these were guests, not staff, so there wasn't much she could do.

"I wonder what she thinks of you and me staying in a suite this week," Faith mused.

Laura's eyes widened. "We're staying here?"

"Yes. Brooke too." Drawing her farther away so as not to disturb the listeners, Faith filled Laura in on the plans for the week.

Laura bounced on her heels in excitement. "When can we get into the suite? Tonight?"

Faith had thought she would move into the manor the next morning, since she'd only learned about Charlotte's offer that evening. "If the suite is empty, I don't see why not."

"I'll check after the show," Laura said.

After locating a couple of empty chairs, they settled in to watch the rest of the performance, which included a juggler, a comic vignette performed by Viola, Corin, and Griffith, and the release of balloons at the stroke of midnight.

While a delicious supper was rolled out, Faith and Laura went to the front desk, snagging smoked salmon rillettes, goat cheese tartlets, and other tasty treats along the way.

Brooke, a jester cap perched on her head like the other servers, intercepted them. "It's not a totally traditional menu," she said in response to their compliments. "But there was a shortage of eel and swan."

"Ugh, I'm glad." Laura wrinkled her nose in disgust, obviously not realizing that Brooke was joking. She popped a mini quiche into her mouth. "This will do just fine."

"We're going to see about moving into the suite tonight," Faith told Brooke. "Do you want to do that too?"

Brooke was silent for a moment. "I'll have to run home and pack. And of course Diva and Bling will need to come along." Diva and Bling were Brooke's beloved angelfish. "The neighbor who usually feeds them for me is away for the holidays."

"We'll let you know what the front desk says," Faith promised. "I'll have to go home and pack a bag too." One of the perks of Faith's librarian job was living in the charming gardener's cottage on the manor grounds.

At the front desk, Cara confirmed that the William Shakespeare Suite was indeed free. "You can check in now if you want," she said, her fingers flying on the computer keys. "Mrs. Jaxon told me you'd be staying in there. Lucky you."

"I agree, lucky us," Faith echoed. Grabbing a piece of manor stationery, she jotted down a list of what she'd need to bring. Watson's kibble, canned food, and treats were on the top, of course. Happy cat, happy life—that was her motto.

Faith and Laura each took a key, and Cara promised to give Brooke one also when she had a chance to pick it up.

After collecting her outerwear, Faith detoured through the library to check on her snoozing feline. After promising to be right back, she slipped through the terrace door and out into the storm.

A gentle thud of footsteps woke the cat. He yawned and stretched, his paws reaching for the fire. The flames had died to coals, the large log now split into glowing pieces.

"Aren't you sweet?" With a rustle of fabric, a woman sat beside him on the settee, pushing him aside with her rather large skirts. She reached out a hand and stroked his head.

She was pretty good at petting. She didn't give the world's best scratches like his human, but she would do. The cat lifted his head for another caress. He rolled onto his side so she could reach the length of his back and batted her hand with a paw.

The human giggled. "So playful." She withdrew the hand and got up to retrieve a small bag on his human's desk. "Would you like a treat?"

He jumped to a sitting position, recognizing the aroma. Tunaroons, made by his owner's friend. She also gave him painful shots, but the cat preferred to focus on her good attributes. He sniffed at the savory nuggets, which made his mouth water.

But something made him stop. How could he be sure if this human had good intentions? His owner always talked about being cautious. So he contented himself with swiping at the treats, sending them soaring toward the carpet.

"You're so silly, kitty." The human watched while he continued to play with the morsels. "I hope we can be friends. I don't have any here, you know." She sighed. "Actors. So self-absorbed. Sometimes they go too far. Do you know what I mean?"

The cat hardly listened as he attacked a tunaroon, then sent it flying.

"I'm afraid someone is going to get hurt. And there's nothing I can do about it."

He launched a treat toward her shoe. Perhaps eating one would make her feel better. It often worked for him.

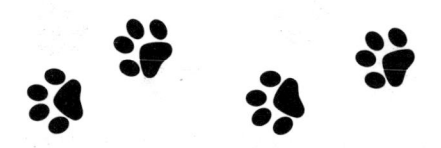

The garden paths, usually kept clear, were already coated with snow. In contrast to the clear sky earlier, thick clouds lowered overhead, spitting down twirling, dancing flakes. Faith trudged along, grateful for her boots and warm clothing.

Although she knew the route by heart, the occasional lights were welcome, their glow like beacons guiding her along. She smiled at the strange shapes the topiaries made, the abstract leafy sculptures grotesquely enlarged by a thick layer of snow.

A tall figure loomed out of the snow, shapeless and dark, features hidden by a hat and a muffler.

Faith's steps stuttered. Who could be out walking this late? Although not a fearful person by nature, Faith had the good sense to be cautious when alone at night in an isolated location.

She picked up her pace again, glancing over her shoulder to watch the other person.

To her surprise, he stopped and lifted one arm. "'But, soft! What light through yonder window breaks? It is the east—'"

Faith burst out laughing. "Wolfe? Are you practicing?" Not that he would be playing Romeo. She'd seen in the production notes that the part was reserved for Griffith.

His arm dropped. "Faith?" Wolfe shuffled forward, the deep snow cresting against his boots. "I didn't see you."

"Apparently not." She snickered to herself. "Though you sounded great."

"It's very kind of you to say that." Wolfe bowed. "Are you headed home?"

"Sort of. I'm on my way to the cottage to pack. We decided to move into the suite tonight."

"Allow me to escort you." Wolfe soon reached her side.

They strolled in silence for a few minutes.

"Walking through a snowstorm at night is an underrated pleasure," he commented.

Faith took in the flakes softly spiraling down to join the shadowy landscape. "Not by me. I love these gardens in every season and at every hour of the day."

Wolfe turned toward her, his features barely discernible in the dim light. "How poetic. I couldn't have said it better." He drew in a deep breath of frosty air. "I've traveled all over the world, but as they say, there's no place like home."

His home since childhood and now mine as well. When Faith had first moved from Boston, she couldn't believe that the grand manor, the magnificent grounds, and her own cozy little cottage were to be home, but now she couldn't believe that she'd ever lived anywhere else. "There's the cottage. I'm so glad I remembered to leave the outside light on."

She found her keys and unlocked the door. "Do you want to come in, or are you headed back?"

He kicked his boots against the stone step. "I'll wait if you don't mind. I want to make sure you get safely back to the manor."

Her heart warmed at his offer, but at the same time, it would be hard to concentrate on packing with him there. It really wasn't a big deal if she forgot something anyway. She could walk over anytime. "How about making us tea while I get ready? I have decaf," she said as she went inside.

Wolfe followed. "No problem." He unwound the muffler and hung it on a peg along with his hat and coat. He ran a hand through his unruly, snow-dampened hair with a grin. "Go ahead and do your thing. I can find my way around the kitchen."

"Sounds good. I'll be packing." She dug in her pocket for the list she'd started, then went into the bedroom and found a duffel bag in the closet. As she packed, she was conscious of Wolfe's movements in the kitchen—the slam of a cupboard door, the creak of his footsteps, the whistle of the kettle.

And an abrupt shout.

3

Faith raced into the kitchen, still clutching her toothbrush. "What's wrong? I heard you yell."

Wolfe seemed to be in one piece, standing in the kitchen holding two mugs.

"Sorry." He set the mugs on the counter. "I saw a strange face in the window, and it startled me."

"A strange face?" Faith repeated.

With two long strides, Wolfe covered the distance to the back door and wrenched it open. He leaned outside, craning his neck to peer into the darkness. He shut the door firmly. "No one is out there now."

Faith hovered by his side. "Can you describe the face you saw?"

"It wasn't human." Wolfe shook his head as he poured boiling water into the mugs. "Maybe I imagined it. Saw my reflection or something."

"That's happened to me." She tried to lighten the mood. "Of course I often look pretty terrifying, especially in the morning."

"You? Never." As Wolfe set the mugs on the table, he motioned to the toothbrush Faith was still holding. "Were you planning to defend me with that?"

Faith laughed. "No, I had it in my hand when I heard you shout."

After she retrieved milk, sugar, and two spoons, they sat down at the table.

Faith poured milk into her mug. "I'm almost ready to go. My clothes are packed, and I just need to gather up some cat food. Milk?"

He added a spoonful of sugar to his tea. "Please."

As Faith pushed the pitcher toward him, she noticed an unearthly visage appearing in the window over the sink. Her hand lurched and the pitcher fell over, sending a river of milk toward

Wolfe's lap. She jumped out of her chair and rose on shaking legs. "Is that what you saw?"

He leaped to his feet to avoid the dripping liquid and whirled around. "Yes," he answered as he dashed toward the door and darted outside.

Now that she had a second to reflect, Faith recognized the mask. It was white with a long beak, often used in Shakespeare plays during costume balls. It also had the more ominous meaning of referring to the costume of so-called plague doctors during that time.

"Come say hello," Wolfe said outside the open back door.

A second later the phantom figure stumbled through, wearing a black cloak that starkly contrasted with the white mask.

Faith braced herself, not enjoying the eerie sight. "Can you please take that off?"

The mask went up, revealing a pretty young woman with freckles across her nose and large hazel eyes. "I didn't mean to scare you."

"Well, you did." Faith gestured at Wolfe. "Him too."

She clasped her gloved hands. "I'm so sorry. I was only having a bit of fun." She had a slight English accent. "I'm Nell Bartlett, one of the players."

"So I gathered," Wolfe said drily. He shut the back door. "I'm Wolfe Jaxon, and this is Faith Newberry."

Nell gave a start, probably recognizing the manor owner's name.

"We were just sitting down for a cup of tea," Faith said. "Would you like to join us?"

"No, thank you. I'd best be off. I wanted a stroll about the grounds. They're so lovely in the snow. But it's late." Nell set her mask back in place and flitted out the back door, closing it quietly behind her.

Faith and Wolfe regarded each other for a moment before bursting into laughter.

"It's going to be an interesting week," Faith remarked.

Wolfe stirred his tea and tapped the spoon on the rim. "You can say that again." His smile was crooked. "I hope I don't make too much of a fool of myself onstage."

"I'm sure you'll be fine." Faith didn't doubt it. Wolfe had enough magnetism and charm to cover a multitude of mistakes if he happened to make any. She was grateful she wasn't being asked to perform. An occasional lecture was enough public speaking to suit her, thank you very much.

"At least I don't have many lines," Wolfe said. "In *Hamlet*, I have two roles, the ghost of Hamlet's father and Polonius, Ophelia's father."

"I sense a theme here," she teased. "Two older men."

"Typecasting at its best," he said with a grin.

They sipped tea in silence, the only sound the ticking of sleet against the windows.

Faith's mind drifted to the upcoming plays. She assumed Charlotte's friendship with the director had led to this unusual event at the manor. "I understand Bates is a friend of your mother's," she said.

"He was my late uncle's good friend. The pair of them used to tease my mother." Wolfe smiled. "The pesky younger sister, you know."

"I'm well acquainted with pesky younger sisters," Faith said with a laugh. "I have one of my own."

They finished their tea in companionable silence.

"I suppose we'd better get going," Faith said reluctantly. "It's late, and we have a play to rehearse tomorrow." Usually she turned into a pumpkin well before midnight, but she could sit up all night chatting with Wolfe.

Wolfe sighed. "I suppose so." He pushed back his chair and stood. "I'll clean up while you finish packing."

"Thank you." Faith smiled to herself, watching him wash the cups by hand while she filled a tote with Watson's food. For a businessman with international connections, he was refreshingly down-to-earth.

"I think I have everything," she announced. The manor provided litter pans so she didn't need to bring one. She set the tote beside her duffel of clothing.

Wolfe wiped the last mug and set it in the cupboard, then hung up the dish towel. "'Once more unto the breach.'"

"You're full of Shakespeare quotes tonight," Faith said. She slipped on her coat, gloves, and hat, then picked up the tote because Wolfe had already chosen the larger bag.

He held the door open for her. "'Brevity is the soul of wit,' they say."

She laughed, then ducked her head against the onslaught of snow and wind. The storm had intensified, and the lights were mere blotches in a world of white.

"Follow me. I could find my way across this land blindfolded." Wolfe winced as driving pellets struck his face. "Which we might as well be."

"'Lay on, Macduff,'" Faith replied, throwing out a quote of her own. Trusting his guidance, she trudged across the gardens behind him, slightly sheltered by his broad figure.

After what seemed an eternity, the lighted bulk of the manor rose up, a welcome oasis in the howling night. They tramped to the terrace and entered through one of the French doors.

When Wolfe shut the door, the absence of sound in the deserted Great Hall Gallery struck Faith's ears like a blow. A few lights still burned around the vast room, but the guests and troupe members were either gone or tucked in for the night.

"I'll walk you up." Wolfe's voice dropped to a whisper.

Faith patted her pocket, feeling the room key safely in place. "Thanks. I'm already checked in. But first we need to get Watson."

As they trod across the empty gallery toward the library, movement on the balcony caught Faith's eye. But when she stopped and stared, squinting into the shadows, she didn't see anything.

She shook her head, thinking she was imagining things. They

dropped the bags by the door, and Wolfe unlocked the library with his set of keys. Inside, all was dark, the fire almost totally out.

"Watson?" Faith called, rewarded by a brush of fur against her ankles. "Come on, Rumpy. We're staying here tonight." Eager to get settled, she picked him up and carried him toward the door.

Something crumbled under her boot, startling her. The sensation was repeated with the next step. What on earth was all over the floor? Wolfe was waiting, so she decided to let the mess stay until morning. *Well, later in the morning.* The clock in the lobby was now striking two.

Wolfe carried the duffel and tote since Faith had Watson. They took the elevator, both too tired for the stairs, and rode to the second floor. Wolfe and Charlotte stayed on the third floor in the private Jaxon apartment.

Wolfe led the way down the carpeted corridor to the Shakespeare suite. He set the bags down and waited while she unlocked the door. Once she had it open, he said, "Good night. Sleep well."

"Thanks. You too." She let Watson down, and he darted into the room. Then she grabbed her bags and slipped inside.

"Faith?" Brooke stood in the doorway to the other bedroom, dressed in a pair of flannel pajamas with a fish design.

"We thought you'd never get here." Laura, blonde hair standing on end, appeared behind her. She wore a pale-blue robe over matching pajamas.

"I had to go back to the cottage and pack," Faith explained. "I ran into Wolfe in the garden, and he came to the cottage for a cup of tea." Her cheeks heated up at this admission.

Brooke rested her hands on her hips, her expression knowing. "No wonder you were gone so long."

Faith refused to respond to that. Instead, she took in the room, which was decorated with a huge canopy bed, a carved wardrobe, and a lady's fainting couch. The color scheme was deep red, creams, and dark green. It felt cozy yet luxurious. "Where's the pet bed?"

"Over there." Brooke pointed to a corner of the room beyond a tall chest of drawers.

"Rumpy, come see where you're sleeping," Faith urged. He'd probably end up with her, but he could at least try the adorable replica of the big bed.

Watson trotted over and sniffed around the bed. Then, to her surprise, he climbed onto it and curled up.

"Something strange happened." Laura shivered, rubbing her arms with her hands. She took a tiny step into Faith's room. "In *this* room. That's why I'm sharing with Brooke."

"So you left the scary room for me?" Faith laughed. She dragged her clothing bag over to the wardrobe and took out her toiletries and nightgown. The rest could wait until tomorrow.

She was on her way to the bathroom when an eerie, high-pitched howling sound echoed through the room. Faith dropped her toiletry bag.

Watson peeked out from his bed, ears pricked.

Laura clutched at Brooke. "There it is again. Isn't it creepy?"

Faith picked up her bag and went to the tall windows. "It must be the wind. It's really blowing out there." The sound reminded her of wind whining around the eaves. But those were one story up. Would they hear it down here?

"Maybe." Laura plucked at her bottom lip, obviously unconvinced. "I thought it sounded like . . . a ghost."

"I've worked at Castleton for years. The manor isn't haunted," Brooke said firmly. "Come on. Let's get to bed. We have a busy day tomorrow."

Laura started to follow. Then, with one last nervous glance over her shoulder, she said to Faith, "You can sleep in here with us if you want."

"I'll be fine." Faith continued into the bathroom to wash up. She smiled when the adjoining door shut with a *click*.

She and Watson would have to deal with the ghost on their own.

Due to the festivities the night before, nothing was scheduled until eleven the next morning. Faith woke at ten, noticing two things right off. First, sunshine was pouring through the curtains she'd neglected to close, indicating the storm was finally over. And second, Watson was lounging on the pillow beside her, his stub of a tail tickling her nose.

Gently pushing Watson aside, Faith slid out of bed and padded to the window. She opened the curtains the rest of the way, immediately squinting due to the blinding white world staring back at her. The small balcony outside her window had to be heaped with over a foot of snow.

Blinking, Faith turned from the view and headed to the bathroom for a shower. She was almost there when the connecting door opened, revealing Laura, her blonde hair tufted like feathers on a baby bird.

Laura put a hand to her heart. "Good. You survived the night."

Although she was creaky with exhaustion, Faith burst into laughter at Laura's melodrama. "If you were that worried, why did you leave us in here?"

Confusion crossed Laura's face. "But you insisted on staying in this room." She took a few cautious steps across the carpet. When nothing happened, she began to stride with more confidence. "After brunch, they're rehearsing *Hamlet*, right?"

Relieved to drop the topic of the mysterious sounds, Faith nodded. "While the actors do that, we'll be helping Audrey and the carpenters with the stage and props. It will be a busy day."

The troupe had their own sets, cleverly crafted for use in all the plays. Today the panels would be put in place in the Great Hall Gallery, along with the lighting and sound systems.

Brooke burst out of the other bedroom, adjusting her blouse as she rushed toward the door. "Good morning." She patted her hair into place. "Goodbye. See you at brunch."

"Talk to you then," Faith called.

Brooke paused in the doorway to the hall, catching herself on the jamb. "Laura, can you please feed Diva and Bling? I forgot."

"Of course," Laura said. "A couple of pinches of food, right?"

"Right." Then Brooke was gone, her footsteps thudding down the corridor.

Faith moved toward the bathroom again, this time resolved to take her shower. "We can go eat together. Wait for me in your room, okay?"

Laura, who was now patting an appreciative Watson, abandoned that pastime and scampered toward her bedroom. "I'll be ready in fifteen."

It was closer to half an hour by the time Faith, Laura, and Watson went down to the main floor.

As they headed to the banquet hall, Laura peered around near their feet. "Where's Watson? I think we lost him."

"He'll turn up." Faith was used to the tuxedo cat's habit of wandering off and exploring.

Inside the banquet hall, long tables held waffle makers, an omelet station, and platters of sausage and bacon. Members of the troupe, many looking the worse for wear after the late night, milled around and filled their plates.

"Coffee first," Faith declared. With Laura at her heels, she made a beeline to the urns, where Wolfe was filling a cup. "Good morning," she said.

Wolfe smiled at them. "Good morning to you. You slept well, I trust?"

"We did, except for the ghost in the Shakespeare suite," Laura said. "Which ancestor do you think it is, Mr. Jaxon?"

"How about pouring us cups of coffee?" Faith asked Laura before she could say anything else about a ghost.

When Laura was carefully dispensing hot brew into a mug, Faith said to Wolfe, "We heard a strange whistling sound in the suite. I think it was the wind." She lowered her voice. "But Laura's convinced the suite is haunted."

Wolfe grinned. "What an imagination. This is an old house, and old houses make strange noises. Even one as well maintained as Castleton."

Laura carried two cups over to them. "Where shall I put these?"

"Find us a seat," Faith answered. "I'm going to get an omelet. And maybe a Belgian waffle too."

"I love the waffles," Laura remarked before walking over to an empty table.

Wolfe raised his cup of coffee. "I already ate, so I'll see you later." He made a comical face of alarm. "After rehearsal."

Faith gave him an encouraging smile. "You'll be fine."

After an unusually large and rich meal that stuffed Faith to the gills, she and Laura went out to the Great Hall Gallery to check the progress on the stage.

A raised platform had been built at one end. Electricians were installing hanging lights, which could be accessed from the balcony. To the left of the stage, two other workers were creating a curtained wall. Faith guessed this was so the cast could slip back and forth unseen from the music room, which had been appropriated for dressing rooms and backstage activities.

Audrey, the stage manager, was standing near the action conferring with Len Britt, the young man in charge of the light and sound panel. She spotted the pair and came bustling over. "Good afternoon. You're Faith, and you're . . . um, Lana?"

"Laura," she corrected. "I'm so excited to be included in this production. What can we do to help?"

"Let me think." Audrey scratched her wild curls, her gaze flitting around the area.

The electricians, under the direction of Len, had finished and were now descending their ladders. A rumbling sound echoed from the lobby, and a couple of staff members appeared, pushing long racks of costumes.

Audrey waved a hand and ran off, shouting, "No, not in here! Those need to go into the music room through the other door."

"There's a lot going on." Laura turned to watch behind them, where chairs were being set up in long rows for the audience. "You'd never know it was a holiday today."

Faith had barely considered the fact it was indeed New Year's Day. A brand-new, unblemished year stretched ahead of her. She hadn't even made any resolutions yet. Not that they usually lasted past February. "Let's go wait in the library," she suggested. "Audrey can come get us when she's ready."

"You know what's really annoying?" Laura huffed as they walked toward the library. "Audrey forgetting my name."

Faith foraged for her keys. "It happens. I forget the names of new acquaintances all the time."

"That's just it. We've known each other for a long time."

"Really?" Faith stood back to let Laura enter first. Then she remembered Laura waving at people on the balcony.

Laura headed for the fireplace, where again one of the staff members had kindly built a fire. "I grew up in Turners Mills, and my older sister was in the same class as Audrey, Griffith, Corin, and Shaw."

"I didn't know they grew up there," Faith said. "It's really interesting that they ended up in the same theater troupe. Well, except Shaw." Griffith's reaction to the Castleton employee now made sense. Apparently, there was bad blood between them.

"I'm guessing they either formed the troupe together or referred each other." Laura picked up a dustcloth and began polishing the elaborately carved mantel and fireplace surround. Although the staff cleaned the library, she seemed to take special pride in taking care of it between their visits. "I know they were all trying to make a go of it in New York, which is tough."

"So I've heard." Faith examined the carpet, remembering that she'd stepped on something the night before. She found what appeared to be pieces of cat treats. Where had those come from?

Faith swept up the crumbs, then made a circuit of the library, checking to be sure all the rare and valuable books were still in place. She lingered for a moment, studying the *First Folio* through the glass. "Come see this, Laura. Bates Beaumont lent it to our library."

Laura tucked away her cloth and joined Faith at the case, admiring the rare work and asking questions about its history.

Not for the first time, Faith reflected on the joy of having the college student occasionally working as her assistant. Laura was open-minded, curious, and a sponge for knowledge.

Brooke popped her head into the library. She wore a little velvet cap, another medieval touch. "Mulled cider and snacks are out in the hall. Coffee and tea too, of course."

Faith groaned. "I can't eat anything after that delicious brunch. But something hot to drink sounds good."

"I could go for some cider," Laura said.

"I'd better get back to work. See you later." Brooke waved and left.

Faith and Laura walked out into the Great Hall Gallery. The cast was taking a break, and they were already gathered around a long table near the stage. Faith spotted Wolfe, deep in conversation with Bates and Audrey.

Shaw, a tray held high, marched across the hall, intent on delivering his cargo to the food table.

A certain black-and-white cat appeared out of nowhere, darting in front of the young man.

Faith saw the disaster coming. "Watson, no!" she cried.

But he didn't respond.

The server tripped over Watson, who had somehow gotten tangled in his legs. The cat yowled, the loaded tray went flying, and Shaw landed on his side with a thud.

Faith was shocked. It wasn't like Watson to be so careless.

Gasps filled the hall, and the onlookers froze.

Wolfe ran forward first, then skidded to a stop when someone shouted, "Watch out!"

One of the hanging stage lights crashed to the floor, right where Shaw would have been if he'd kept walking.

4

Someone shrieked.

As if released from a spell, Wolfe dashed toward Shaw. As he passed a couple of staff members, he said, "Please clean up this mess."

They scurried to obey.

By the time Wolfe reached Shaw, the young man was sitting up and checking himself over.

"Are you all right?" Wolfe asked him.

"Yeah." Shaw rubbed the shoulder he'd landed on. "I'll be black-and-blue for a while, but I'm fine."

As for Watson, he skirted the room, weaving between people and furniture until he reached Faith.

She crouched to pick him up. "Rumpy, you bad boy. You know better than to do that. What got into you?"

In answer, Watson blinked, appearing satisfied.

Had he—? But no. How could he have possibly known the light was going to fall and land on Shaw? Craning her neck, Faith examined the scaffolding above the stage, where the now-vacant space was clearly visible. Cats did have sharp senses, and perhaps he'd seen or heard the light working its way loose.

Or maybe someone had... Faith pushed the suspicion aside. Yes, the light was close to the balcony, but she hadn't seen anyone up there before the accident.

Watson struggled in her arms so she released him. He scampered off.

Shaw was now on his feet, helping the others clean up the spilled food.

Wolfe, Audrey, and a shaken Len headed toward the stairs to check out the lighting situation.

Brooke sidled up to Faith. "Someone's going to be in trouble. They didn't install that light correctly, and now they're going to have to check each one."

Laura returned from the drinks table with two mugs of hot cider. She handed one to Faith. "A server said she saw someone up there right before it happened." She shook her head. "Get this. The person was wearing the bear suit."

The bear suit was a costume for *The Winter's Tale*.

Her remark sent a charge through Faith. "Do you think someone did it on purpose?" She glanced up at the balcony again and recognized Nell, who was making her way toward the grand staircase. She liked to dress up, judging by the mask she'd been wearing the previous night.

Brooke snorted. "I'd take their stories with a grain of salt. The staff is always coming up with wild theories. I didn't see anyone up there, let alone a bear."

As Corin walked by them, he stopped and gave a start of recognition. "Laura, what are you doing at Castleton? I haven't seen you in ages."

The young actor, while not as obviously handsome as Griffith, had his own charm. Most startling were his pale-green almond-shaped eyes.

Laura blushed. "I work here. And I'm finishing up my college degree."

His attention was apparently on other things. "Great to hear. See you around." Corin strode across the floor toward Viola, who was laughing at something Bates had said.

Audrey clattered down the stairs and marched up to Faith and Laura. "I can use your help now," she announced, running her hands through her tangled locks. "Can you please check the costumes and sort them by actor? There are costumes for the staff too. Those can be handed out."

Brooke took advantage of the interruption to slip away, giving Faith a look that meant they'd talk later.

"Is there a list of who is wearing what?" Faith asked. She'd seen the racks of clothing, and sorting them appeared to be a daunting task.

"Yes, of course." Audrey pointed vaguely toward the music room. "There's a system. You'll see." She stared up at the stage. "I've got to make sure the scaffolding is secure. We were lucky once. We might not be so lucky next time," she added as she walked away.

On the way to the music room, Faith and Laura passed Shaw, bringing another tray of food into the room.

"I'm glad you're okay," Laura said.

"Me too." Shaw grinned. He was a tall, strapping young man with a square chin. His mop of dark curls fell into his eyes no matter how often he tossed his head, which was quite often. "That cat came out of nowhere. And I'm sure glad he did. Otherwise that light would have beaned me good."

"That's Watson, and he belongs to Faith." Laura made introductions.

"Laura got me the job here," Shaw said. "I really appreciate it."

Laura flapped her hand at him. "Think nothing of it. I didn't make the hiring decision." She nodded toward the stage. "We'd better get going. We've got costumes to sort."

"See you later." He gave them a mock salute before ambling off.

Faith avoided walking under the lights as they made their way around the stage. Behind the curtain they followed the route the actors would take back and forth from their dressing rooms.

The racks of clothing filled the middle of the quite large music room. Except for the grand piano, the furniture had been moved out, and temporary walls had been put up to make two dressing rooms.

Faith found the costume binder on a folding table littered with play-related materials. As Audrey had said, there was a system. Inside was a list for each actor with costume numbers, also organized by play. She sighed when she saw that the costumes were stuffed onto the racks in apparently random order. They had a big task ahead of them.

Laura flitted about the room, poking her nose into the trunks and boxes of props, hats, and footwear. She opened a large leather trunk and leaped back with a yelp.

"What is it? A body?" Faith asked drily. The trunk was certainly large enough.

"Almost," Laura said, laughter in her voice. She reached inside the trunk and removed a skull, then cradled it in her hands. "Meet poor Yorick."

The sight made Faith drop the binder, and it crashed to the floor. As she bent to pick it up, someone gasped behind her.

Faith spun around to see Marlene.

"Put that down," Marlene ordered.

For a second Faith thought she meant the binder. Then she noticed that Marlene was glaring at Laura.

"It's disgusting that these actors are using *human* remains," Marlene sneered.

"What kind of remains should they use?" Laura asked innocently, still holding the skull. "At least we're not doing the play that has a severed head as a prop. Though I'm sure they'd use a fake one in that case."

Marlene obviously wanted to give Laura an earful but managed to refrain.

"Were you looking for something?" Faith asked, hoping to guide the conversation onto a more pleasant path.

Marlene swiveled toward Faith. She bit her lip, swallowed, and said in a surprisingly calm tone, "I'm here for my costumes. Mrs. Jaxon insisted I wear medieval garb along with the rest of you." Her sniff expressed what she thought of that idea. But Marlene respected Charlotte and would never criticize her verbally.

"Let's see if we can find them." Faith led the way to the rack holding staff clothing. To her immense relief, she saw it was organized by name. She located Marlene's outfits. The assistant manager had a dress for each performance night and the gala to be held on the last night of the event.

Laura set down the skull and joined them. She pulled out the first of Marlene's dresses, a vision in blue brocade trimmed with gold lace. "Wow. You're going to be gorgeous in this."

In a rare display, Marlene's cheeks pinked. "You think so?" Curiosity in her eyes, she began to leaf through the gowns. "This may not be so bad after all."

"Has anyone seen Wolfe?" Perdita Beaumont stood in the doorway, wearing a one-piece rubberized suit and booties.

"Mr. Jaxon is in a meeting," Marlene answered. "I'll inform him that you'd like to speak to him. May I ask what it's about?"

Perdita gathered up her loose hair and tucked it under an orange hat. "I just returned from frostbite sailing, and I need to talk to him about my boat, which is down at the dock."

"Why on earth would you go sailing on a day like this?" Laura blurted. "It's barely ten degrees out there."

Marlene furrowed her brow, but she didn't reprimand Laura, probably not wanting to draw attention to her ill-chosen words.

But Perdita didn't seem to notice or care. "The water was quite toasty in comparison. I sail year-round, every day if I can." She turned on her heel and disappeared.

"Better her than me," Laura muttered when Perdita was gone. She shuddered. "You wouldn't catch me out on the ocean in the winter."

"That may be true. But please remember to be discreet." Marlene tapped a finger on her lips. "No criticism of retreat guests, please. No matter how bizarre they may act."

Laura ducked her head. "Yes ma'am." She collected Marlene's dresses, holding them by the hangers. "Are you taking them with you now?"

"Have them sent to my suite, if you would." Marlene's smile was crooked. "I'm staying here this week too."

"Isn't it a treat?" Faith commented. "We're enjoying the Shakespeare suite."

"Except for the ghost," Laura said. "I'll call the front desk and get someone to drop off your dresses, Ms. Russell."

Marlene ignored the ghost remark. Instead, she nodded. "Thank you. I'll see you both at dinner. It's in the Jaxons' apartment tonight." She strode toward the door, her steps brisk.

"See you later, Marlene." Was the woman actually mellowing? Faith could hardly believe it.

After Laura arranged for the gowns to be delivered to Marlene's room, she joined Faith at the long racks.

"Let's get started on the costumes," Faith said. "I have a sneaking suspicion we're going to be here all afternoon."

They worked efficiently for a couple of hours, with Faith calling out numbers and Laura moving the costumes to the right racks.

Audrey popped in around four o'clock when an early-winter dusk was falling. "How's it going?"

"Great. We're almost done." Faith gestured toward the racks, where Laura had created cards with actors' names in different colors to easily delineate groups of outfits. "Laura is wonderful at organizing."

Audrey wandered over and examined a few costumes. "Nice job. I think these are in pretty good shape. But they'll need to be dry-cleaned after this set of performances."

Laura pulled out a pair of breeches. "Well, we might have one problem."

"What do you mean?" Audrey asked. "Those look fine to me."

"This is one of Mr. Jaxon's costumes. See how wide they are in the waist?" Laura held them up to demonstrate. "Obviously the other actor was a little heavier."

Audrey took the breeches and studied them, frowning. "You're right. We need a seamstress. Any thoughts?"

Faith had an idea. "My aunt Eileen lives in town. Maybe she can do some alterations for us." Hopefully Eileen was getting over her cold.

"Do you mind calling her to see?" Audrey asked.

"Not at all," Faith replied. "When do you need Wolfe's costumes altered?"

"The day after tomorrow. That's when we're performing *Hamlet*." Audrey ran both hands through her curls, a gesture she seemed to make often, and gave a huge sigh. "There's always something, no matter how well you plan."

Her comment reminded Faith of the stage light mishap. "Did you figure out what happened earlier when Shaw almost got hit?"

Audrey groaned. "Did you have to bring that up? What a nightmare. We examined the rest of the lights, and they're fine. In fact, we added extra wire to make sure."

"That's good." Faith was relieved that the actors wouldn't have to keep checking overhead for falling equipment. "I'll give Aunt Eileen a call right now."

Faith dug her phone out of her bag and dialed Eileen. Her aunt was feeling much better, and she was more than eager to help. Faith disconnected with a glow of satisfaction. It would be fun to have Eileen around this week. "She'll be here tomorrow morning."

"Great. Thank you." Audrey ducked out.

Once again, Faith and Laura were alone with the costumes.

"I think we're done here," Faith said. "Why don't we take our outfits upstairs and freshen up for dinner?"

They called the front desk for help, and one of the staff members showed up a few minutes later with a luggage rack. They loaded their clothing on it and wheeled it to the elevator. Then Faith and Laura pushed the rack to their suite.

Night had fallen, and the hallways were dim, lit by ornate sconces.

Faith unlocked the door and entered the suite, fumbling for the switch.

In the slanting light from the hallway, she saw a furry face with gleaming eyes staring back at her, huge teeth bared.

5

Faith jumped backward into the hallway. "There's something in there!"

"Come on. Let's get out of here." Laura broke into a run, pushing the rack in front of her.

Faith followed. With each step, she calmed down a little more. After all, nothing was chasing them. Furry face, teeth—it added up to one thing. "Laura," she called, "I think it's okay."

Laura halted abruptly, the clothing swinging on the hangers. "Really? But you said—"

"I think it's the bear costume. Someone put it in our room to scare us." Faith went back to the room, still cautious enough to push the door open fully before stepping inside.

The two-part bear costume had been propped on a chair facing the door, placed to greet anyone who entered.

Faith waited for Laura to return before going all the way inside. This time she quickly found the overhead light switch and turned it on.

Laura sucked in a breath, one hand over her mouth. "I can see why that scared you, especially in the dark. Who put it in here?"

"I have no idea," Faith said. It was obviously someone who had managed to get a room key, because she was certain she'd locked the door.

Laura sighed. "I suppose we should report it to Ms. Russell, but I really hate to do that."

Faith did too, considering Marlene seemed to be enjoying the event. Or more accurately, she was on the verge of doing so. Why risk spoiling that?

"Let's wait and see if something else happens." They could leave the bear where it was for now and put it back with the rest of the costumes in the morning. She refused to give the culprit the satisfaction of letting him or her know they had been startled.

Watson slipped through the open door and made a beeline right to the bear. He sniffed its feet briefly, then proceeded to rub against Faith's ankle, giving his feed-me-now meow.

"Rumpy has spoken. He's not too worried about it." Faith laughed. "One dinner coming right up."

After feeding her pet, Faith took a quick shower and dressed for dinner. She chose pants in winter-white wool and a soft sweater with a blue-and-white pattern.

Laura slipped into a long skirt and a ruffled blouse. Then she pinned her hair up and added a touch of lipstick.

"You look so cute," Faith said as they went to the elevator. They'd decided they were too tired to walk up a flight of stairs. "I like your hair in a bun."

"Thanks." Laura gave her a shy smile. "Hopefully I put in enough pins. My hair is so fine and flyaway."

Faith had been in the Jaxons' apartment on a number of occasions, so she led the way to the dining room.

The theater troupe was already gathered there, with Brooke and Shaw serving the food. At first sniff, Faith identified savory beef stew. Side dishes included fresh rolls, vegetables, and salads. She and Laura joined the line, which moved along both sides of the buffet table.

"May I interest you in wild beast stew, milady?" Griffith bowed elaborately, gesturing for Viola to proceed to the buffet table ahead of him.

She wrinkled her delicate nose. "Wild beast? What are you talking about?"

"Perhaps they shot it out on the grounds," Nell put in. "As Robert Frost said, 'The woods are lovely, dark and deep.'"

Corin gave her a thumbs-up for the apt words.

"I was only making a joke." Griffith turned his back on the actress and snatched a bowl off the stack.

As for Viola, she studied the food offerings with a touch of dismay.

"I promise we use only the finest domestic meat," Wolfe told Viola from the other side of the serving table. "Brooke assures me this is grass-fed and free-range beef."

"And local," Brooke said proudly. "Like most of our food."

"Decades ago, Griffith might have been right," Charlotte added. She was obviously attempting to smooth things over. "Your grandfather was quite a hunter, Wolfe. Deer, pheasant, and duck ended up on our table."

"Seriously?" Viola bypassed the stew and served herself a pile of vegetables.

Behind Viola, Corin ladled stew into a bowl. When Shaw came up beside him, he started and slopped gravy onto the white tablecloth.

"Don't mind me," the server muttered, swapping out baskets of rolls. "Just making sure everything is all set."

With a frown, Corin grabbed two rolls and propped them on his bowl. "It appears to be." He hurried to keep up with Viola, then steered the actress to a seat at the table.

Griffith, who'd evidently kept a chair empty for her, scowled. Audrey slid into the vacant seat. Bates sat on the other side of Viola and immediately engaged her in conversation. Corin glared, clearly wanting to monopolize the actress's attention. Nell sat beside Corin and began talking to him, although his gaze never left Viola.

Laura had been watching the actors. "This is like a preview. Or a prequel."

"Or a soap opera," Brooke whispered, reaching between Faith and Laura to refill the peas. "Talk about drama kings and queens."

"I suppose that's appropriate," Faith said. She preferred a drama-free life, but she had to admit the troupe's antics were rather fascinating. After selecting her meal, she joined the others at the table, taking a seat beside Bates.

"Your portrayal of Ophelia is really shaping up," Bates told

Viola. "In fact, it reminds me of a rather remarkable performance I saw once—oh, where was it?" He shook his head. "Never mind. It will come to me."

Nell's expression was jeering. "Lucky Viola. She's already getting accolades, and we haven't even gotten out of rehearsal."

Viola's gaze jerked toward Nell. "Don't start. We all get equal billing here."

"Not exactly." Corin's lip curled. "Griffith gets all the starring roles."

Griffith popped a piece of bread into his mouth, seemingly unperturbed by the other man's animosity. "There can be only one Romeo. But the role of Count Paris isn't bad."

Corin jumped to his feet, his bowl of stew swaying dangerously. *Is he doomed to spill gravy everywhere?* Faith wondered.

Corin rested both hands on the table and leaned toward Griffith. "I challenge you to a pool tournament. Tonight after dinner." Apparently he'd heard about the rule against dueling. "Winner plays Romeo."

Griffith scoffed. "You're kidding. *Romeo and Juliet* is only a week away. How on earth would you pull that off?"

Corin straightened, putting one hand to his heart. Staring at Viola, he said, "'It is my lady, O, it is my love! O, that she knew she were! She speaks, yet she says nothing: what of that?'"

"Stop it!" Viola yelled. Her cheeks flushed deep pink when she noticed everyone staring at her. "We get the point, Corin."

"So are we on?" Corin glanced around the room, then pointed at Shaw and Wolfe. "Do you guys play? We'll do teams."

"Count me in," Wolfe said. "I play a mean game of pool."

"As do I," Bates said. "But before you decide to cast my plays using cue sticks and billiard balls, shouldn't I be consulted?"

"Don't worry. The lineup will survive intact." Griffith crossed his arms and gave Corin a theatrical glare.

Corin laughed in mockery. "I wouldn't be so sure. Pride goes before a fall, remember."

"And what of us women?" Nell rested her hands on her hips, pouting. "Shall we battle for Juliet?"

"No way." Viola lifted her chin. "I'm not giving that up."

In the end, two teams were formed, led by Griffith and Corin.

Faith didn't want to play pool, but after dinner she and Laura went along to the billiard room with the others. Bates decided to retire, as did Charlotte, but Wolfe was drafted for Team Corin.

Brooke and the servers set up hot and cold beverages and decadent desserts on a sideboard, perfect for grazing during the evening.

As a somewhat macabre touch, someone fetched poor Yorick from the dressing room. Used as a mascot of sorts, the skull was parked at one end of the pool table or the other, depending on which team was winning at the moment.

Len, the audio technician, set up a small camera to film the action. Faith noticed the move encouraged greater theatrics and over-the-top reactions from the players.

"Are you sure you don't want to sub in?" Wolfe asked Faith after a few games. "We could use your help."

"You don't want me. I'm terrible at pool." She stretched her feet toward the fire, basically immobilized by the cozy heat and the comfort of the goose-down-stuffed leather armchair. Watson sat in her lap, purring. "Besides, I'm content right here." She scratched Watson's chin. "Or should I say we are content."

Wolfe stepped closer to the hearth and stared into the leaping flames. "I don't blame you a bit. It's that kind of night. Temperatures are down in the single digits."

Faith shivered at the thought, grateful she didn't have to brave the cold to reach her bed. It was right upstairs, waiting for her.

There were shouts and groans as someone sank the last ball of a game.

"Break," Griffith called.

There was a clatter of cue sticks as the players dropped them on the table and swarmed toward the refreshments.

"The score is two to two," Corin announced. "The next game determines the winner. Which will be me." He clasped both hands overhead in the classic victory gesture.

The others responded with jeers, hoots, and cries of "Good luck!"

Shaw picked up Yorick and chased Nell and Viola with him.

The women shrieked with laughter as they raced to escape.

"Unhand my head," Griffith said, referring to his role as Hamlet. "That is so undignified." He began handing out bottles of drinks to the others.

Audrey took colas for herself and Shaw and popped the tops.

"Want something to drink?" Laura asked. "I'm going up." She levered herself out of the chair next to Faith, where she had been reading on a tablet.

Faith regarded the beverage selection. She noticed an urn of spiced cider warming on the sideboard next to the other drinks. "Bring me a mug of cider, please," she said.

Perdita drifted into the room, resplendent in a flowing green dress. She perched on a sofa near Faith and smiled. "What did I miss?" For once the woman didn't appear sulky or aloof.

"Multiple rousing games of pool," Wolfe spoke up from his position by the fire. "Did you get your boat all taken care of?"

"Yes, thank you." Perdita's eyes glowed with warmth. "Your dockmaster was such a help. Glenn and I put it on a mooring so I can go out again tomorrow or the next day."

"Good to hear." Wolfe held his hands out to the fire, turning them as though toasting them. "I love sailing, but I've never ventured out in the winter."

Perdita gave a little bounce on the couch. "You should definitely try it." Her voice held the fervor of a zealot. "It's a magical experience. At the same time, it really tests your skills and stamina."

"I'll bet," Wolfe said. "In these temps, the wrong move could be deadly."

Perdita thrust out her bottom lip. "Phooey. You just have to dress properly."

Laura returned, handing Faith a mug and sitting down with a can of ginger ale. "Miss Beaumont, I was so impressed with your *First Folio*. I've never seen anything like it."

Laura's tact diverted Perdita from her main passion, and she started waxing on about the volume of plays.

Behind them, the young men were horsing around. Something crashed, and Nell cried out.

Faith whirled around to look. Shaw stood beside an accent table that had fallen over. A vase lay on the floor, somehow unbroken, though its dried arrangement had spilled out.

"Sorry," Griffith said to Wolfe. "It was an accident." He bent to pick up the vase while the others gathered the foliage and flowers.

Shaw leaned against the wall, putting both hands to his head. "I don't feel very good."

Wolfe moved quickly across the carpet. "Did you hurt yourself, Shaw?" He glanced around at the others, who all shook their heads.

"I don't see how," Corin said. "He didn't fall down."

"Are you ill?" Wolfe asked.

"I'm okay," Shaw insisted. "Just tired. Time to go home." He headed for the door, moving slowly.

Wolfe picked up the house phone and spoke into it. When he hung up, he said, "We're having someone run him home. I don't want him driving."

His thoughtful gesture warmed Faith's heart.

"Now who are we going to get to play?" Griffith asked. "We're down a person."

Wolfe glanced at Faith, who shook her head. She shifted in her chair, feeling only slightly guilty.

"I'll do it," Laura volunteered. She set aside her ginger ale and stood.

"Can we take another break first?" Nell asked.

As though released by the departure of Shaw and Nell, some of the others, including Perdita, wandered out.

Griffith and Corin urged them to hurry back.

"If we don't play that last game," Griffith said, "then the role is still mine."

Corin pretended to consider it. "I don't agree. In that case, we'll have to find another way to break the tie."

Faith's eyes met Wolfe's.

He shook his head slightly and gave a small smile.

She knew he felt the same way. The actors' rivalry was amusing as long as it didn't hamper the production.

Perdita burst into the room, waving both hands wildly. "Help! Somebody help!" She stopped and panted for breath. When she could speak, she said, "It's Shaw. Something's wrong with him."

"What's wrong?" Wolfe asked.

Perdita sagged against the doorjamb, eyes glistening in her stark white face. "I found him lying on the floor."

"Show me," Wolfe said. "The rest of you stay here, please." On his way out of the room, he said to Brooke, "Call 911."

While Brooke picked up the house phone and called emergency services, the actors clustered together, murmuring and questioning each other.

Her pleasure in the fireside gone, Faith got out of the chair, wishing she could help somehow.

A muffled sob caught her attention.

Laura was hunched over, a hand to her mouth. "Poor Shaw. Just when he was getting it together."

"He'll be all right." Faith knew her words were hollow, but what could she say? She crouched down and put an arm around Laura. "Wolfe will make sure he gets the best medical attention." That was true at least.

"The ambulance will be here in a few minutes," Brooke announced as she hung up the phone. Then she slipped out, no doubt to give Wolfe the update.

"No, you don't understand. Shaw has health issues." Laura tapped her chest. "His heart isn't good."

Faith stood. "You think he's having a heart attack? I'd better tell Wolfe." This information could mean the difference between life and death. She tugged at Laura's arm. "Come with me. You may be able to help your friend."

The others watched as Faith and Laura—and Watson—left the room, but no one followed.

They found Wolfe kneeling near Shaw while Brooke and Perdita looked on.

Shaw lay prone on the hallway carpet. His skin was gray and his breathing labored.

Wolfe glanced up at them, his expression grim. "I think he's in a coma."

"He has heart problems," Laura blurted. "I'm not sure exactly what they are, but he takes medication."

"Good to know," Wolfe said. "Every little bit helps."

Faith noticed a crumpled ball of paper on the carpet, resting near Shaw's hand. She stooped to pick it up, and out of curiosity, she smoothed it out. *Speak me fair in death*, it read. She gasped.

Wolfe and the others turned to her.

"I found this on the floor." Faith read the quote. "Do you think it belongs to Shaw?"

Consternation flowed over Wolfe's features. "I sure hope not."

"It's from *The Merchant of Venice*," Perdita said. "We're not doing that play this time." She raised her nose in the air. "Though I thought we should."

Faith's fingers tightened on the paper before she realized that she'd probably obliterated any fingerprints. She slipped it carefully into her pocket, out of instinct more than anything. Shaw's heart was acting up, right? It was a medical emergency. That was all.

Wolfe glanced down the hallway at the sound of voices and rolling wheels. "Here they come." He released a long breath of relief.

The little group watched as the efficient paramedics assessed Shaw and then loaded him up for transport to the hospital.

Wolfe passed along the information about Shaw's heart, and Laura added that Shaw was under the treatment of a local physician.

"He's in good hands now," Wolfe said, watching as the gurney trundled down the hall, gently guided by the EMTs.

Laura threw herself into Faith's arms. "Oh, I hope he'll be okay."

Faith patted her softly on the back. She hoped so too.

6

After the paramedics left, Faith and Laura decided to go up to the suite. Neither felt like sitting around with the actors and hashing out the frightening situation.

Bates Beaumont, dressed in a silk smoking jacket over flannel slacks, met them on the stairs. "I saw the ambulance. What's going on? It's not—"

"Perdita is fine," Faith assured him. "I'm afraid that Shaw Hastings has taken ill. He's on his way to the hospital."

Bates furrowed his brow in obvious confusion.

"He's the one who almost got hit by a falling light earlier today," Laura said.

The juxtaposition of the two events struck Faith as odd. But surely one was an accident and the other—well, the doctors would make that verdict.

"He did have a bad day," Bates muttered. "I'm very sorry to hear the news." He grabbed the polished rail. "Now that I'm up, I might as well grab a hot drink."

"There are drinks and desserts in the billiard room," Faith said. "Good night."

"A good night to you too," Bates replied as he descended the stairs.

Faith and Laura continued to the second floor.

"I'm exhausted," Laura said, moving her feet as if they were encased in cement. "I can't wait to go to bed."

"Rest up," Faith said. "We have rehearsals all day tomorrow." They had barely achieved the top when she remembered something. "Where's Watson?"

Laura peered down the staircase. "I thought he was right behind us."

"So did I." Faith sighed. "I'd better go round him up. I don't want him wandering around all night."

The cat stalked the couple down the hallway, crouching low and darting behind furniture when they turned his way. Once in a while he liked to do this in order to keep his prowling skills up to snuff. It was part of his training regimen.

"I do hope Shaw is going to be all right," the woman said. "I can't imagine what happened."

"With Shaw? It could be anything." The man snorted. "He's always been a troublemaker."

"That's rather callous of you," she said sharply. Then her voice softened. "But I understand why you don't like him."

"No, I don't. Not that I wish him ill, of course." He sighed. "I hate having the past rear its ugly head again."

"Me too."

They walked in silence for a minute.

The cat practiced getting really close without being noticed. To his pleasure, he realized that his paws made no sound on the thick carpet.

"I guess we're in the same boat now, relationship-wise," the woman said, tossing her hair. "How does it feel?"

The man stopped abruptly, and the cat dived behind a chair. "It's not the same at all. I want to marry—"

Judging it was now safe, the cat emerged from hiding and began slinking along the baseboard. Once again he wanted to see how close he could get.

"Marry her?" The woman's laugh was bitter. "You never felt that way about little old me."

"That's not fair. I told you from the beginning that it wasn't serious between us."

She stared at him. "'The most unkindest cut of all,'" she quoted. She spun on her heel and ran down the corridor. Right toward the cat.

He froze. He was stuck with no place to hide.

Then he saw the window. And the curtains.

Faith couldn't believe her eyes. As she came down the hallway, Watson jumped down from behind a set of curtains, which meant he had been perched on the sill or on top of the sash. "Rumpy, what were you doing in that window?"

A terrible thought crossed her mind. Heart in her throat, she went to the curtain and examined it for claw holes. Relief washed over her when she didn't see any.

He sat at her feet and gazed up at her, as though to say that she should trust him.

With a laugh, she bent down and scooped him up. "Time for bed. And I'm going to make sure you stay with me this time."

"Faith?"

An urgent voice roused Faith from a very deep sleep. She opened her eyes and saw Laura hovering over her, tears streaming down her face. Faint gray light around the curtain revealed that it was early morning.

"What is it?" Faith's heart kicked into gear, and she jolted upright, dislodging an irritated Watson.

In answer, Laura plopped onto the bed, putting both hands to her face. "It's Shaw." Sobs shook her shoulders. "He's . . ."

Dread pooled in Faith's limbs. She could guess where this conversation was going. "Is he gone?" she whispered.

Laura nodded and hurled herself into Faith's arms.

"Oh, I'm so sorry." Faith put both arms around the distraught young woman.

Brooke slipped out of the other room, her face somber. "I heard the news." She was already dressed. "I'll go down and get breakfast for us."

"I can't eat," Laura wailed. She pulled away from Faith and fumbled for a tissue in her robe pocket. "I'm devastated."

Sensing her distress, Watson crawled into her lap.

"You have to eat something to keep up your strength." Faith's eyes met Brooke's. "We'll take coffee and toast. Maybe some scrambled eggs. Thank you."

"I'll be back soon." Brooke walked out, the door closing almost soundlessly behind her.

Laura repeatedly stroked Watson's back, and the cat patiently endured the attention. "I got a call this morning from Shaw's brother. He promised to keep me updated since the hospital wouldn't tell me anything." She paused to blow her nose. "They said it wasn't his heart."

A lance of shock ran up Faith's spine. So Shaw's death might not be from natural causes. "Do they know what happened?"

Laura shook her head, then sniffed. "Not yet. I guess they're going to do more tests." Glancing toward the door, she asked, "When do you think Brooke will be back? I think I'm actually hungry after all."

Marveling at the resiliency of youth, Faith watched Laura eat two helpings of eggs and four pieces of toast. Then they showered and dressed. Before joining the others in the Great Hall Gallery for the rehearsal of *Hamlet*, they took a detour with the bear costume and returned it to the dressing room.

The troupe was gathered around the stage, scripts in hand. Perdita, sipping from a cup of coffee, sat in the audience, and Len was at his station, ready to run lights and sound. Faith and Laura took seats in the second row.

Bates stood onstage, already addressing the actors. "As usual, we'll do a run-through from the top, no stopping. Then we'll assess and go back over scenes that need more work. It's not like you haven't performed this before." His gaze fell on Wolfe. "Well, most of you."

Wolfe grimaced. "I'll try not to bomb too badly."

Everyone laughed.

"There's one more thing before we get started." Bates cleared his throat. "We had some bad news this morning. Castleton has lost a fine young staffer. Shaw Hastings." He lowered his head.

Laura's hand crept into Faith's.

Faith squeezed the young woman's hand and studied the group, who reacted with various degrees of surprise. Audrey's face reddened, and she appeared to be fighting back tears. Viola's mouth hung open, but her eyes were dry. Griffith studied his fingernails. Corin huffed out a breath and shook his head. Nell's lively face was somber for once.

Wolfe appeared pained, and Faith knew how hard this must be for him. He regarded Castleton employees as an extension of his family, no matter the length of their service. With a lift of his chin, Wolfe set his shoulders in determination, a visual cue that he would follow the right course of action, no matter how difficult.

Her boss's integrity stirred warmth in Faith's heart. The longer she knew him, the more deeply she admired him.

After about a minute of silence, Bates cleared his throat again. "Let's get started. Places, please. Scene one."

Each play had been condensed down to one act, which Faith thought amazing. Some of the minor roles had been telescoped into one, and the actors took on these parts as they could, sprinkled among their main roles.

As for Wolfe playing the ghost, he was dignified and grim as he intoned the lines with portentous gravity. Once finished with his scene, he sent Faith a look, raising his brows as though to inquire her opinion.

She gave him a big smile and a thumbs-up.

They were about halfway through the play when Marlene entered the Great Hall Gallery, her heels clicking on the marble. Behind her were Chief Andy Garris and Officer Bryan Laddy.

At the sight of the police, Faith's hope that Shaw's death was merely an unfortunate tragedy evaporated.

"I'm sorry to interrupt," Marlene said. "But Chief Garris needs to speak to everyone who was here last night."

"I guess the show won't go on," Nell quipped, earning both smirks and glares.

Laura leaned against the wall beside Faith with a groan. "This is not good news."

"No, it's not." Faith put an arm around her friend, anxiety bubbling in her belly. Then she whispered, "As the Bard said, 'The game's afoot.'"

"Good morning, Faith," Chief Garris said. "Please sit down."

The chief and Officer Laddy were seated in the den located next to the library.

"Good morning." Faith took the chair opposite and folded her hands on the tabletop. She'd been near the bottom of the list, with the actors and crew questioned first. Laura and Brooke were still waiting, although Marlene had insisted they keep working until they were interviewed.

Faith and Laura had spent the interrupted morning making sure the actors were all set with costumes. When Eileen had arrived to work on Wolfe's outfit, she'd been stunned to discover the police there.

Her aunt's words still rang in her ears. *I can't quite get my mind around it. Between the time you called me yesterday and this morning, a young man has died and the police are investigating?*

Faith shifted in her seat. Apparently, that was the way things worked at the manor.

"All right," Garris said, "let's go through the events of last evening."

As the chief asked questions, Faith told them all the details she remembered from the time the group had gathered in the billiard room to when Shaw collapsed.

"Tell me," Garris said, his blue gaze sharpening. "Was any food served? Or beverages?"

This seemingly innocuous question set off a bell in Faith's mind. Did they suspect poison? But how could that have happened? They'd all been grazing on the snacks Brooke had provided. And the drinks were mainly bottled or canned.

She said as much. "I remember Griffith opening sodas and handing them out. But they were capped until then." She leaned forward. "Do you think someone poisoned Shaw? I don't see how they had a chance. We all ate the same food, and the drinks were sealed. Except for the coffee, which again, none of us got sick from drinking."

Officer Laddy, who had been silent until now, replied, "Let's just say Mr. Hastings ate or drank something he shouldn't have. We're trying to narrow down the possibilities."

That definitely sounded like poisoning to Faith. But who was responsible? She supposed Shaw could have done it to himself. Or it might have been an accident, something that reacted with his medicine. If only she knew what toxin they had found. She thought about asking but decided they probably wouldn't release the information. The last thing she wanted to do was annoy the chief.

"Is there anything else you want to tell us?" Garris asked. "Did you notice anything out of place or odd last night? Or since Mr. Hastings started working here?"

"Actually, yes." Faith reached into her pocket and slid the slip with

The Merchant of Venice quote across the table, glad she'd thought to keep it with her. "I found this in the hall near where Shaw collapsed. I don't know if it's his for sure, but it seems strangely appropriate." She gave a half-hearted laugh. "No use dusting it. I put my mitts all over it before I realized."

The chief read the note, his brow crinkling. Then his expression cleared. "Shakespeare. Any member of the troupe could have dropped it." He handed it to Laddy.

"That's true. But I think it's too much of a coincidence that it was beside Shaw's body. I think he had it. Maybe it fell out of his pocket." Faith remembered what Perdita had said. *We're not doing that play this time. Though I thought we should.*

"He could have—" Laddy bit off his words when his boss glanced at him. "We'll keep the note." He tucked it into an evidence envelope and wrote the relevant information on it with a marker.

"Is there anything else?" the chief asked Faith.

She shook her head.

Garris turned to Laddy. "Are we all set?"

The officer capped the marker. "Good here, Chief."

Garris nodded. "Thanks for your help, Faith. If you think of something else, any detail from last night, please let us know."

She rose from the table. "I'll do that." The clock on the mantel struck noon. "Would you like something to eat? I can ask Brooke to bring you lunch."

"Sounds good to me," Laddy said immediately. "That breakfast sandwich I had this morning is long gone."

Garris cracked a brief smile. "Lunch sounds good, if it's not too much trouble. Thank you."

Faith walked toward the door, relieved to have the interview over.

She had her hand on the brass knob when Garris called, "And, Faith? Hopefully we'll get this wrapped up quickly. But until then, be careful."

7

Eileen Piper regarded her niece, her eyes wide with concern. "The chief warned you to be careful?" She tsked as she set her sewing aside. "I don't like the sound of that."

Faith hadn't either. "It seems like they think it was murder." She lowered her voice although she and her aunt were alone in the dressing room. "I don't see how or when it happened with a roomful of people. But obviously the police know more than I do."

"How is Laura doing?" Eileen picked up the breeches and began hemming again.

Faith got up from her chair and wandered over to the costumes. Their bright colors and rich fabrics drew her like a moth to a flame. "She's really upset. When she woke me up this morning, she was in tears."

"Was she close to Shaw?" Eileen paused her stitching to study her work.

"I'm not sure." Faith flipped through the costumes, straightening sleeves and twitching skirts into place. "They grew up in the same town, Turners Mills, and Laura helped him get a job here."

"Hmm." Eileen picked up a pair of scissors and snipped the thread. "But his death is upsetting anyway, of course. Laura is such a sweetheart. I'm so sorry this happened."

"Me too. It's awful." Restless, Faith abandoned the clothing and scanned the hats and other accessories placed on a long table. For fun, she plopped a triangular horror with dangling veils on her head and checked her reflection in a standing mirror. "Oh my."

Eileen laughed when she glanced up and saw Faith in the ridiculous headgear. "I think you might have to go sideways through the doorway with that on." She threaded the needle and began stitching again.

Brooke popped her head around the doorjamb. She reared back when she saw Faith's hat. "That's certainly a showstopper."

Faith laughed as she plucked the monstrosity off her head.

"Lunch is ready in the breakfast room if you're interested," Brooke said. "Soup buffet and make your own sandwiches." Small groups often ate meals in the breakfast room.

Eileen set her sewing on the table and stood. "Brooke, how are you?"

"Okay, I guess." Brooke made a face. "I just finished talking to the police. That wasn't a whole lot of fun."

"Tell me about it," Faith said. "Did you see anything strange last night that might help them?" She fell into step with Eileen and Brooke as they made their way to the breakfast room. From the music room, they could cut straight through the salon, the shortest route.

"Not really," Brooke replied. "There was so much going on. I was focused on the game, not watching people's every move."

They reached the breakfast room, and Brooke politely stood back to let Eileen and Faith enter first. She chuckled. "It doesn't look like the interrogations affected anyone's appetite." She hurried off to talk to one of the servers, who was carrying in a tray of cookies.

Members of the troupe were clustered around the buffet, and despite the small crowd, the room echoed with their chatter. Charlotte was seated beside Bates at a four-top table with Viola and Wolfe.

Faith and Eileen went to the buffet and checked out the vats of soup. The choices included seafood chowder, beef barley, and chicken potpie, with mini biscuits floating on top.

"This is a hard decision," Eileen said. "But I'm going for chicken. Nothing like comfort food on a cold winter day."

Faith had to agree. She had a bone-deep chill from the terror of dealing with Shaw's death. "Chicken sounds good. And we won't even need a sandwich with those biscuits."

Eileen ladled two big bowls full, and they carried them to a large table. Faith poured them each a glass of water with lemon from the pitcher already on the table.

Eileen sat facing the doorway. "There's Laura," she said and waved.

Laura waved back on her way to the buffet.

"Is this seat taken?" Corin asked. Without waiting for an answer, he set down his food and sat across from Faith.

"Please do sit with us," Faith said, hiding a smile.

Next, Griffith, Audrey, and Nell joined them at the table. Fortunately, there were still two seats left, so Laura would have a place to sit.

Once they were all settled, Faith introduced them to Eileen.

"It's nice to meet you all," Eileen said. "I'm a big fan of the theater, so I welcome the chance to volunteer."

"If you need any adjustments or repairs to your costumes, Eileen's your woman," Audrey said. "Right now she's taking in Will's outfits for Wolfe."

"That's a lot of work," Griffith cracked, his mouth twisting. "Will is a, er, fine figure of a man."

Corin snickered.

Nell swallowed a mouthful of chowder, then groaned, putting a hand to her midriff. "I'm glad you're here, Eileen. If I keep eating like this, I'll need all my seams let out."

With a lifted brow, Corin regarded her bowl of soup and sandwich with chips. "You might want to cut back on your portions there, tubby."

Faith cringed at the remark.

But Nell brushed it off. "It's natural to eat more in cold weather," she said in her charming accent. "It's a survival mechanism."

"I wonder how much she eats then," Griffith said, motioning to Perdita, who entered the room wearing her sailing gear. "Sailing in winter temps has to burn tons of calories."

"Better her than me," Corin said, eyeing Perdita's outfit. "She's always been strange." He picked up half of his sandwich and demolished most of it in one bite. "How do you all think the rehearsal is going so far? Will we be ready for tonight?"

As Corin and the others conferred about the play, Faith focused on her meal. The chicken soup was rich and satisfying, and there were plenty of vegetables and chunks of meat. The kitchen crew was definitely on top of their game this week.

Laura set a bowl of soup on the table and slid into the empty chair beside Faith. "Hello, everyone." She turned to Eileen. "Nice to see you again."

"Same to you." Eileen's brow creased with concern. "I was so sorry to hear about your friend."

Laura kept her attention on her soup as she dipped her spoon into the broth. "Thanks. It's been hard."

Perdita stopped by their table. "Have you all spoken to the police?" She pulled out the last chair and sat down. "I can't believe the direction the questioning took. I thought he died from a heart attack." She patted her chest to illustrate.

An odd glint came into Griffith's eyes. Elbow propped on the table, he held a sandwich with one hand while picking up chips with the other. "Maybe he finally did away with himself." He popped a chip into his mouth and crunched.

Audrey winced and dropped her spoon with a clatter. She picked it up and chided, "That's an awful thing to say."

Griffith shrugged. "He had issues. You know that." He smirked at Corin. "What do you think? You and Shaw were real close in the old days, right?"

Faith glanced at Laura, concerned about how she was taking this insensitive banter.

Laura had set down her spoon and was sitting very still, staring at Griffith. But Faith sensed coiled energy behind the quiet. Laura was waiting to strike, much like Watson with his chosen prey.

"We were in the same class at school," Corin answered, "but we weren't close."

"But you hung out with him. I remember that." Griffith wouldn't let the subject go. The intensity of his gaze reminded Faith of a dog with a bone.

Corin pushed his chair back as though preparing to get up. "Sure. But once Shaw got in trouble, it was better to distance myself." He lowered his voice to a deep, resonant tone. "Ditch the loser."

Laura slapped her hand on the table, a sudden move that made several people jump. Even the people eating at Wolfe's table glanced over.

"Hold on," she said, her voice low and furious. She leaped to her feet, leaning on the table with both hands. "Slandering a dead man who can't defend himself? You should be ashamed of yourselves."

The troupe members stared at her in shock.

But Faith enjoyed a surge of righteous satisfaction at the well-deserved reprimand. A glance at Eileen confirmed that her aunt was on the same page.

Before anyone could respond, Laura whirled around and marched out of the room.

Everyone turned to watch.

"Whoa," Corin said. "What was that?"

Griffith chuckled. "I had no idea she was such a fiery one."

Neither did Faith. But she also hadn't been aware that there had been so much animosity between Shaw and his old friends. Perhaps *friend* wasn't the right word. These people acted more like his enemies.

She couldn't help but wonder why.

After lunch, Faith found Laura upstairs in the suite, sprawled on her bed, crying.

Watson was curled up next to her, providing his own brand of comfort.

"I'm so sorry," Laura said when she saw Faith. "I didn't mean to cause a scene." She shuddered. "Marlene is going to kill me."

"Marlene wasn't there, and I'm not telling. And if they tell her, I'm sure Wolfe will back you up." Faith sat on the armchair next to the bed. "I don't blame you a bit for being angry. So was I, and I barely knew Shaw."

Laura rolled onto her side and reached for a box of tissues on the nightstand. She appeared marginally less upset, although red blotches still flamed in her cheeks. "It's so awful."

Faith thought about how to broach the subject of the troupe's attitude toward Shaw. "Not to pour salt in the wound, but why do you think they have so much animosity toward Shaw?"

Laura balled up her used tissue and tossed it into the wastebasket. "I don't know the whole story. But I do know Shaw got in trouble and had to go to a juvenile detention center. Something about a prank gone wrong."

"It sounds like they still resent him for it." Faith thought about that. "It's been—what, ten years?" She guessed the troupe members were all in their midtwenties.

"I think they're mean bullies," Laura said stoutly. "Why can't they let someone move ahead from their past? That's what Shaw was trying to do."

"And it was admirable," Faith said. Surely if anyone deserved a second chance, it was a teenager.

Laura burst into tears again. "He wanted to go to college," she choked out between sobs. "He was saving money for tuition."

Faith shook her head, wistful over the young man's lost opportunity. Now the world would never know what Shaw might have done with his life. "What do you think happened? A person with goals isn't likely to kill himself."

Laura sniffed, dabbing at her eyes. "I don't think so either. And despite what they said, he didn't have issues." She stared into space for a moment. Then her mouth dropped open. "Do you think someone *murdered* him?"

"It seems like the likeliest option. But we'll have to wait and see what the police come up with." Faith stood. "I'd better get downstairs. Why don't you take the afternoon off? I'll clear it with Marlene."

Laura scrambled off the bed. "No, I'd better stay busy. Lying up here brooding won't help anything."

They went back downstairs to learn that the rehearsal was picking up where it had left off. Audrey assigned Laura to help with wardrobe changes during the play, along with Eileen, who volunteered. Faith was in charge of props, making sure each scene and play had the proper ones onstage.

After the rehearsal, Laura went to help Eileen with the ironing and newly discovered costume problems.

Faith decided to go to the library for the rest of the afternoon. On the way, Watson appeared out of nowhere and followed her.

A roaring fire provided cheer, and Faith could feel the comforting warmth all the way from her desk. She sat in the chair with a sigh, realizing how long it had been since she'd worked in undisturbed peace.

Watson settled in his usual spot on the settee.

Fifteen pleasant minutes went by. Then the library door rattled open.

Faith suppressed her irritation and put a welcoming smile on her lips. She reminded herself that her real job was to help guests and staff.

Bates shut the door behind him and strolled inside. "Ah, good afternoon. Don't let me disturb you. I'm just here to visit my *Folio*." Apparently a man of his word, he moved directly toward the case and stood in front of it, hands clasped behind his back.

Now Faith's smile was genuine. She could relate to the idea of someone visiting a book as if it were a person. Books were precious things that held a spark of life, even if made only of leather and ink and paper.

Now the door opened again. This time Perdita entered. For a change she was dressed in normal clothing—a pair of jeans, a thick sweater, and fleece-trimmed boots.

"Back already, my dear?" Bates asked his daughter as she joined him. "How was the sail?"

Perdita blew out a breath. "I didn't get very far. The winds were gusting up to twenty-five knots, and it wasn't safe to go out."

"Don't worry. I heard it will calm down tomorrow." Bates continued to study the book, seeming to bask in the sight of it.

Perhaps if Faith owned such a valuable book, she'd bask in the sight of it too.

"Maybe so. But it will be snowing." Perdita's tone was sharp. When her father didn't respond, her annoyance seemed to subside. After a couple of minutes, she said in a low voice, "You know what tomorrow is, don't you?"

For the first time, he turned to regard her. "Of course I do. How could I ever forget your mother's birthday?" His voice held a note of reproach.

Perdita's mouth opened and closed a couple of times. "Well, you don't ever say anything. And you're always too busy to talk to me about her." Her voice became louder with every word. "Too busy spending time with your new protégé, Viola," she spat. "Maybe you should send me away again so you'd have even more time with her."

Bates sent Faith a pained look. "Perdita, please."

His daughter rested her hands on her slim hips. "What are you worried about? I'm not ashamed of what I'm saying. Mama is dead, and I'm the only one who cares. And no one cares about me or my life."

"That's not true at all." Bates put an arm around his daughter's shoulders. "Let's go discuss this somewhere else," he said between clenched teeth. "This is a library. We need to keep quiet."

Perdita shrugged off his arm. "Why? There's no one in here. It's like any other room." She cupped her hands around her lips and shouted, "Can you hear me?" Her voice echoed, bouncing off the thirty-foot ceilings.

Faith reached for the phone on her desk, although she hated to do it. But the situation appeared to be disintegrating fast. Perdita was losing control, and Faith couldn't allow that in the library, not while it was under her watch.

Before she could dial, she heard Wolfe call down from the balcony, "I can hear you just fine." He descended the spiral staircase. "Is everything all right in here?"

Faith put the receiver down, enormously relieved to see him.

Perdita gasped. She whirled around and fled from the room.

Bates waited for Wolfe to approach. "I'm so sorry," he said, wringing his hands. "I'd better have a doctor come check her over. I think she's stopped taking her—" He glanced at Faith, his face reddening.

"It's all right, Mr. Beaumont," Faith said. *Now that Wolfe is here.* "We're very discreet at Castleton." She swallowed, then offered, "It seems to me that she's grieving over her mother's death. That's completely understandable." But she'd never seen anyone handle grief in quite that way.

Bates seemed to accept the explanation gratefully. "Yes. Perdita and her mother were extremely close." His expression was bleak. "Perdita wanted me to hire her as stage manager, but I thought she was too fragile. Maybe I made things worse by refusing. It would have given her something else to focus on."

Wolfe clapped Bates on the shoulder. "Why don't you go find your daughter? I'm sure she needs you."

"I'll do that. Thank you." Bates gave them a nod of farewell and strode out of the room.

Once the door shut behind him, Wolfe sighed. "Poor old Bates. He's having a rough go of it."

"I take it his wife died," Faith said. She went over to the fire and poked at the logs.

Wolfe followed and placed another log on top of the coals. "Yes, Imogen died a few years ago in an accident. But she was his second wife. His first wife disappeared."

"Was she murdered?" Faith blurted out. Why did her mind so quickly jump to foul play? She didn't want to consider what that said about her.

Wolfe took the poker from her hand and gave the new log a couple of adjustments. "Not that we know of. Beatrice was a quite famous stage actress, but the stresses and tensions of that life got to her. So she took off without a word. That's what Bates said, anyway."

"I'm sorry to hear it. Now he's lost his second wife, and his daughter is..."

He set the poker back in its stand with a *clank*. "Troubled?" His gaze was thoughtful. "Perdita has always been a bit odd, even before her mother died. The family lived locally for a while, and I remember that she was an emotional child. Years ago when Bates brought her and a carload of her teenage friends over for the day, she was moody then."

"What teenager isn't?" Faith sank down on the settee beside Watson, patting him absently while gazing into the flames.

He rested a paw on her leg, as if letting her know he appreciated the attention.

Faith wondered why people couldn't be as simple as cats. Give them food, fire, and fun, and they were content.

"I had a call from the chief today," Wolfe said. He set his hand on the mantel, standing to face the flames. "He told me that Shaw was poisoned by yew."

8

For a moment, Faith couldn't make sense of Wolfe's words. *Shaw was poisoned by you.* Her mouth opened, denials rushing to her lips. Then she realized. "You mean yew, the tree?"

Wolfe faced her and shot her a surprised look. "Of course." Then he paused. "Though I can see how that could be confusing. I'm sorry."

Faith couldn't imagine anyone eating yew needles inadvertently or on purpose. It would be like chewing on the branch of a Christmas tree. "Shaw didn't eat yew, did he?"

He clasped his hands behind his back. "They found traces of it in his system. They think it was in liquid form, since they didn't find plant matter in his stomach."

She closed her eyes, remembering the scene in the billiard room. "It had to be the soda. But I don't see how that could have happened. The bottle was sealed."

"Unless he set his drink down and someone spiked it." Wolfe pressed his lips together. "They said yew acts rather quickly, so they think it happened here. Plus, he was working at the manor all day."

Faith considered the possibilities. "Do you think he killed himself?" She heard the doubt in her voice. "Some of the actors were bandying that theory around."

Wolfe's smile was humorless. "They would, wouldn't they? No one wants to believe there is a murderer lurking about."

The incident with the stage light popped into Faith's mind. "I just thought of something. Remember when the light fell? What if it was aimed at Shaw?"

Concern filled Wolfe's eyes. "I never considered that. I assumed it was an accident." He reached inside his jacket pocket and pulled out his phone. "I'm going to tell the chief about it." He held his fingers poised over the screen. "But first, tell me what you remember from that day."

Faith did her best to relive that moment in the Great Hall Gallery and gave Wolfe every detail she recalled.

"Good job. You've got a great memory." Wolfe called Garris and filled him in. After a few minutes, he disconnected and slid his phone back into his pocket.

"I guess I've got a good cataloging system up here." Faith tapped her temple. She hoped the information would help the police with their case. "Chief Garris warned me to be careful. So I think they're already leaning toward murder."

Wolfe paced back and forth across the hearth rug, running a hand through his hair and making it stand on end.

She thought about the crumpled note. "That quote I found implied the opposite, though. It made it sound like suicide. What else could 'Speak me fair in death' mean?"

"I found that quote disturbing then, but it's even more so now. Whatever happened, I hope the police get to the bottom of it quickly." He raised an eyebrow. "And do be careful, like the chief said."

"Of course I will. But you never know, we might see or hear something vital to the case." Faith swiftly added, "Quite by accident, naturally."

"Naturally," Wolfe muttered. "Are you available later to help me with my lines? Tonight is my big stage debut." For the first time she could remember, he sounded a bit nervous.

"Do you want to meet back here at six?" she suggested.

Wolfe smiled. "It's a plan." He bent to pat Watson. "Be a good boy and watch over your mistress, won't you?"

Watson's combination meow and yawn made them laugh.

"I think that was a yes," Faith said.

Watson's paws batting at Wolfe seemed to confirm his owner's interpretation.

"He's the smartest cat I know," Wolfe said. "You almost get the sense he understands us."

"There's no 'almost' about it," Faith said.

The phone on her desk rang, and she hurried to answer it.

"Well, I'll leave you to it," Wolfe said, then exited the library.

To Faith's dismay, the caller was Marlene, and she wanted to see Faith in her office immediately.

"What's all this about a murder?" Marlene stood behind her desk with her arms crossed, fuming. "The police are here again, and they're questioning our actors."

Faith plopped down into one of Marlene's visitor chairs without an invitation, a move that earned her a glare. "Wolfe and I were just discussing it. Shaw died from yew poisoning."

Marlene's slender brows knit together in confusion. "Yew? Oh, you mean the tree."

"Right. Apparently it's quite deadly." Faith had taken a minute to look it up online. Every part of a yew was toxic except the pretty red berry flesh. "Sometimes victims die without even presenting symptoms. One man just inhaled yew sawdust and died."

Marlene didn't respond.

When the silence became uncomfortable, Faith cleared her throat. "What did you want to talk about?" Perhaps Marlene merely wanted a handy victim to vent her ire upon. That wouldn't be unusual. The assistant manager regarded any deviations from perfection at Castleton as a personal insult.

Marlene dropped into her desk chair as suddenly as if her bones had dissolved. For a moment, her frigid expression slipped, revealing a deep fatigue.

It has to be hard, upholding her incredibly high standards, Faith realized.

"I so wanted this week to go well. It's very important to Mrs. Jaxon. Mr. Beaumont is one of her good friends."

Faith couldn't argue with that. She attempted a diversionary tactic. "How's your room?"

Marlene's face softened, and she almost smiled. "Pure bliss. Did I tell you they gave me the Jane Austen Suite? She's one of my favorite authors."

This was an unexpected glimpse into Marlene's personality. "Mine too," Faith said, although she regarded the novels of fine literature as if they were her children. How could she choose favorites?

Marlene picked up a pen and twirled it between her fingers. She didn't meet Faith's gaze when she asked, "I was wondering... do you have any theories about this regrettable event?"

"Before I answer that question, I have one for you." Faith thought she might as well take the opportunity to clear—or delve into—one line of inquiry. "How was Shaw doing here? As far as his job was concerned?"

Her first reaction was textbook Marlene. "I can't tell you that. It's a confidential employee matter."

"He's dead," Faith said softly. "Any information that can help needs to be on the table."

Marlene swiveled in her chair. "All right. But don't tell anyone else or reveal that this information came from me. Got it?"

"Got it," Faith repeated. Guilt panged when she thought of her friends. They shared everything. "But what if—"

Marlene raised her hand. "No one," she said firmly.

Faith reluctantly nodded.

Marlene sucked in a deep breath and leaned forward across the desk. "We gave Shaw an employee loan because he was in pretty desperate straits when he started working here. And Mrs. Jaxon believes we should help our people." She sniffed, the closest she would get to a criticism of Charlotte. "A certain amount is taken out of paychecks every week to pay back the loan."

Faith scooted her chair closer. "And?" She thought it was a nice policy, and she imagined it was probably rewarded by fierce loyalty on the part of employees.

"Shaw wasn't cutting it, I'm afraid. As a server, at least. He was clumsy, disorganized, and prone to back talk." Marlene lowered her voice. "We had to put him on probation." She imbued the word with such dire meaning that at first Faith thought she was talking about punishment for a crime.

"Were you going to let him go?" From the way Shaw acted while working, Faith would never have guessed he was in trouble with his job.

"If he didn't shape up, the short answer is yes. But then of course we would have an issue collecting the loan." Marlene shook her head. "We would probably have had to write it off. And now I guess we definitely will."

Faith sat quietly, absorbing this new information. Had the prospect of being fired pushed Shaw over the edge? Maybe the police were on the wrong track, and he had killed himself. She was deeply saddened by the idea.

With a resolute effort, Faith pushed these painful speculations aside. "Do you know anything about Shaw's background? Perhaps the reason for his death lies in something outside the manor."

Marlene pursed her lips. "Of course it does. No one here did anything wrong. You can count on that."

"So you don't know anything that might offer any clues."

"I didn't say that," Marlene responded sharply. "I know he came from Turners Mills. His mother, Evelyn Hastings, still lives there. She was his emergency contact."

Sadness dropped over Faith like a cloak at the mention of Shaw's mother. "Laura told me that he'd been in trouble with the law as a youth. I wonder if something from his past made a return."

"Trouble? How?" Marlene narrowed her eyes. "If it has to do with legal issues, I may be able to help you."

Faith rocked back in her seat, surprised. "Really? I thought juvenile records were usually sealed."

"They are. But if you know the right people, you can find out things." Marlene shrugged. "That's all I'm saying."

Faith knew the assistant manager had some dodgy associates in her past, including her ex-husband. Sometimes Faith wondered if Marlene's rigid ideals at the manor were a way to overcompensate for the sins of her previous life.

Faith pushed herself out of the chair. "Thanks. I'll keep you posted on what we learn." She stepped toward the door, then paused. "I have every confidence we'll get through this. And the manor won't be blemished."

Marlene's response was a grumble, and Faith sensed her walls were firmly back in place. She slipped out of the office.

Faith studied her reflection in the bathroom mirror and added a touch more lipstick. Then she blotted most of it off.

"You look great," Brooke said, leaning against the doorjamb. Her eyes twinkled with mischief. "Wolfe will be impressed."

"Cut it out." Faith examined her outfit. She'd chosen a white sweater featuring a blue Fair Isle pattern on the yoke and her best jeans. Casual but trim. "I'm just helping him with his lines."

"His lines?" Brooke repeated. "Is that what they're calling dates these days?"

"Very funny," Faith said as she exited the bathroom. "I'm not sure how long we'll be." She glanced around the room. "Where's Watson?"

Brooke motioned to the adjoining bedroom. "Snuggled up with Laura. I think you've got competition."

"I'm not worried about it." Fortunately, Faith wasn't the jealous type about her cat, who had a habit of making new friends. In this case, she was sure he was providing comfort to the bereaved Laura. He was good that way.

She checked the clock. "I have a few minutes. Want to catch up? I feel like I haven't had a real conversation with you in ages."

Brooke sat on the fainting couch. "I know. It's been so hectic." She lowered her voice. "Is there anything new regarding Shaw's death? I heard it might be murder."

Faith filled her friend in on everything she could. She'd promised Marlene she wouldn't talk about Shaw's work performance, but of course Brooke already knew how he'd been doing in the kitchen. Fortunately, Faith didn't have to bring it up.

"He wasn't doing so well," Brooke admitted. "He used to butt heads with everyone."

Faith checked the time, not wanting to be late for her meeting with Wolfe. "I'd bet Shaw's death has something to do with his life outside the manor. I hope so, anyway."

"We'll both have to keep our eyes open," Brooke said. "He was a nice guy, if a little immature. He was always broke and hitting people up for money."

Even on top of the employee loan? "He was pretty personable." Faith stood, straightening her sweater. "I'd better—"

An eerie wailing sound interrupted, rising and falling in a downright creepy way.

Laura opened the door to the adjoining room. "There it is again." Eyes wide with fear, she rubbed her upper arms with both hands. "The ghost."

"It can't be a ghost," Brooke said. "Someone else would have reported it before."

Now there's a commonsense explanation, Faith thought ruefully as she darted to the window. She yanked the curtain aside and stared out into the moonlit night. Tree branches weren't moving, so it wasn't the wind. Next she went to the fireplace and peered up inside. "I think it might be air blowing down through the flue." But it didn't seem like the sound was coming from there.

Glancing around, Laura walked into the room tentatively, as if something might explode. "Maybe we should leave. I'm not sure I can take this."

Brooke put an arm around her. "It's okay. It's just a noise." She motioned to Watson as he ambled into the room. "See? He's not scared."

In fact, Watson appeared entirely unperturbed, and beyond a twitch or two of his ears, he ignored the noise. He went to his bowl and began to crunch kibble.

Faith laughed. "Let's take a cue from my cat." As she bent to pat him goodbye, the strange sound died away. "I'll ask Wolfe about it, okay? See you two later."

Wolfe was in the library, tending the fire while he waited. He set the poker in the stand when Faith entered. "Good evening. Ready to teach an old dog new tricks?"

"You're not that old," she said with a grin, crossing the rug to the settee, where two copies of the script waited.

"I'm glad you think so," he said, settling beside her and picking up his script. "Compared to the kids I'm acting with, I'm ancient."

"I know what you mean." Faith sometimes felt almost maternal toward the young workers at the manor, including Laura. She took the other script and scanned the pages for his parts. He'd thoughtfully highlighted them.

He read his first line as the ghost: "'Mark me.'"

Faith read Hamlet's line: "'I will.'" Then she put up a hand. "Why don't you stand and read? You should move around as though you're onstage." She rose. "I'll stand too."

"Good idea." He cleared his throat and began again.

The abbreviated nature of the script meant the scene was over within a couple of minutes. The whole while, his role as the ghost reminded Faith of the strange occurrence in the suite.

"Well done." She smiled and clapped. "But before we go on, I have something to ask you."

Wolfe flipped ahead to the next scene in the script. "Go ahead."

"Remember Laura asking you about a ghost in the Shakespeare suite?"

"Yes. That was hilarious."

"Well, I can understand her thinking now," Faith admitted. "Tonight we heard some very strange sounds in there." She tried to imitate the unnerving sound.

He rubbed his chin. "I can't imagine what would cause that noise."

"At first I thought it might be air coming down the flue."

"There's a metal cap on the chimney," Wolfe said. "On all the chimneys, as a matter of fact."

Faith nodded. "When I went over to the fireplace, it didn't seem like it was coming from there. Maybe somewhere high up on the walls."

A light dawned in his eyes. "Let me check on something. I'll get back to you."

"Thanks. I'll tell Laura you're on the case. She'll be relieved." Faith thumbed through her script, but when she glanced up to look at Wolfe, movement on the balcony caught her eye.

The bear face was peering down at her. She was becoming so used to odd events that it barely caused a quiver.

Before she could say anything to Wolfe, whoever was wearing the costume turned and scurried away. The upstairs door shut softly.

Not bothering to alert Wolfe to the troupe's latest foolishness, she said, "All right. Let's take the next scene from the top."

She'd go up and block the door if she needed to. Anything to keep people out of the library after hours.

"'Alas, poor Yorick!'" Griffith said, holding the skull aloft.

Wolfe as the gravedigger paused to listen.

Faith watched from backstage, enthralled by the play. Despite the glitches and problems—and tantrums among the actors—the performance had come together, and so far, it was superb. By the silence in the audience, she guessed they were equally swept away to long-ago Denmark.

The Great Hall Gallery was in darkness beyond the stage lights, with tall candelabras in the rear and at the exits providing a flickering glow. Fresh garlands and displays of fruit gave the feeling of winter abundance.

Many of the attendees had gotten into the spirit by wearing medieval costumes. Faith wore one of the gowns lent to her. It was made of mauve taffeta with gold accents. The fur trim around the neck and cuffs was especially cozy.

Laura, also dressed in vintage garb, appeared equally caught up. Her lips moved slightly as the actors recited their lines. She reached out and grabbed Faith's arm when the funeral procession for Ophelia arrived at the graveyard. Tears stood in her eyes.

Dear Laura, who wore her heart on her sleeve. But Faith was similarly touched, especially when Griffith's grief appeared to be genuine. He really was an excellent actor. So were the others. Corin was versatile, and Nell was charismatic and compelling. Viola was heartbreakingly beautiful as the tragic Ophelia.

An uneasy thought wormed into Faith's brain, breaking the play's spell. Solving a murder was challenging enough under normal circumstances. But trying to sort truth from lies in a troupe of actors? What a tangled web that might prove to be.

Soon after, the curtains closed to thunderous applause. Then they swept open again, and the cast took their bows.

Perdita swept onto the stage and presented the actresses with beautiful bouquets.

Audrey nudged Faith and Laura. "Come on. It's the crew's turn."

Her belly clenched with apprehension, Faith followed the stage manager into the glare of the lights. Taking a position between Audrey and Laura, she forced a smile onto her lips and curtsied, a beat behind Audrey.

Behind them, Len stood with Bates, and they took their bows.

As she'd done with the actors, Perdita hustled onto the stage and handed each of the women a bouquet.

Under the spotlights, Faith noticed Perdita's skin appeared paler than ever. Sweat stood out on her brow, and her lips were pressed into a white line. She must have hated being on display as much as Faith did.

"Perdita," Bates called, gesturing for his daughter to join him. He put his arm around her and moved forward to the front of the stage, almost pulling a reluctant Perdita along.

Faith and the others moved to the side, opposite the actors, who were clustered together.

Wolfe smiled at Faith, wiping a hand across his brow to convey how relieved he was that his debut was over.

She grinned back and gave him a subtle thumbs-up.

When the applause quieted, Bates said, "Thank you all for your warm reception of our little theater troupe. This is only our second season, and aren't they great?" He motioned to the actors.

The audience clapped.

"You are our first audience in the New Year," Bates continued. "And what a wonderful group you've been."

The crowd broke out into wild cheers.

"My lovely daughter and I thank you, and we look forward to

having you join us for *Much Ado About Nothing*, two nights from now." Bates raised a hand. "Hold on. There's more."

He waited long enough to make Faith squirm with curiosity, and she was sure the rest of the onlookers were too.

"Due to my daughter's hard work, we have an opportunity to be televised live in New York after this run. Producer Sid Meyers is in attendance to see if we're a good fit. So be nice to him, all right?" Bates gave an exaggerated wink.

The crowd chuckled.

Len had darted back to his audiovisual station, and now a light beamed over the spectators, focusing on a man with dark hair and a goatee, his gold-rimmed glasses glinting in the spotlight.

Sid waved and called, "Bribes accepted here."

Laughter and cheers rang out.

As Faith finally left the stage, she reflected that Sid's interest was good news for the troupe. But she couldn't suppress a suspicion that this opportunity had raised the stakes for someone.

Maybe someone who had seen Shaw Hastings as a threat and decided to eliminate him.

9

Later that night at the cast party, the atmosphere in the billiard room verged on hilarity. The actors seemed overjoyed at the prospect of appearing on television.

Faith, tucked in her comfortable seat by the fire, took in their antics. While she was often amused, she also hoped to uncover a clue regarding Shaw's death.

"I thought old Bates was blowing smoke with his television talk," Nell said. "But he produced the goods all right."

Corin bent to make a shot, lining up his stick with the cue ball. "Bates has a stack of television credits, you know. So I had every expectation he would come through."

The cue ball missed the target and dropped into a pocket, creating a scratch.

"Bummer, dude." Griffith laughed. He stepped up to the table and took his turn. "Perdita told me Sid had been calling, so I was expecting him to show up. Good thing I was on my game tonight." He sank a ball. "Like I am now."

Corin lifted his chin and stared at Griffith. "You? I'm amused that you think your performance sealed the deal."

"Boys, boys. Calm yourselves." Viola stepped up to the table. Her shot was flawless, a combo landing in the corner pocket. She blew on the stick. "That's how I roll. Broadway, here I come."

Nell looked the other actress up and down. "Don't count your Tony Awards before they hatch."

Corin hooted with glee, then slung an arm around Viola's neck and pulled her close.

She play-slapped him to get away.

Audrey sauntered into the room, carrying a script. "Hey, everyone." She removed her glasses and waved them by one of the bows, then slid them back on. "Don't stay up too late. We have rehearsal tomorrow at eight." She paused. "In the morning."

This announcement was met with general groans.

"Can't we celebrate a little, boss?" Len asked. He sat at a table fiddling with his video camera. "Sid said he might have room for me on the production team."

Audrey snorted as she joined Len at the table. "Good for you. He didn't make that promise to me." Setting aside her script, she rested her chin on her hand. "What are you watching?"

Behind them, the others continued their billiard game.

Len scooted his chair closer to Audrey. "This is video from the other night." He lowered his voice, but Faith, seated next to them, could hear him clearly. "I want to make a montage with clips from this week."

Faith's ears perked up. Without invitation, she left her seat and went to the table. Standing between them, she asked, "Do you mind if I watch?"

They both gave her puzzled expressions but didn't object, so she grabbed a chair and sat down.

"This is the pool game," Len said. "Look at these clowns."

They watched for a while, Faith studying the interplay captured on video between the troupe members.

Was that a glare from Griffith at Shaw when Shaw was taking a shot? Or was Nell especially snippy at Shaw when he made a corny joke? Faith wished she could get a copy of the video, but there was no inconspicuous way to ask.

On the film, the pool game ended, and the gang took a break. Griffith pulled soft drinks out of ice and handed them to Audrey. They served the drinks to the others in kind of an assembly line.

Shaw pointed to a bottle and said quite clearly, "That one."

Griffith picked it out of the ice and gave it to Audrey, who twisted it open.

Faith's pulse quickened. Was this when Shaw had been poisoned?

As if reading her mind, Len whispered, "I wonder if that's what killed him." He jabbed a finger at the screen at the moment Audrey handed Shaw the open bottle.

"That's not funny." Audrey pushed back from the table and stood so fast the chair teetered on two legs for a moment. Then she bolted from the room.

"Hey, I didn't mean you did it!" Len called.

The actors stopped and stared at them.

"What's going on?" Griffith asked, leaning on his pool cue.

"Audrey thinks I'm blaming her for Shaw's death," Len replied. "Just because she handed him a soda." He shook his head. "In a bottle you gave her."

Griffith's eyes widened. "Whoa. Are you accusing me?"

Corin snickered. "If the shoe fits. Something—or should I say someone—poisoned him."

Griffith set down his cue and pushed up his sleeves, a supremely casual yet threatening gesture.

Faith tensed.

"It wasn't Griffith." Viola pushed herself between the two men. "Cool it, both of you."

"What have I done?" Len stood, waving his camera. "Guys, no one is accusing anyone of anything. We were watching video of the pool game the other night." He pointed the camera at them. "I could shoot this, though. It would go over great on social media."

That threat seemed to do the trick. Both men backed off, allowing Viola to move away.

"I think we should all call it a night," Griffith said. "We've got an amazing opportunity ahead of us, and I, for one, am not going to blow it."

The next morning the bird mask came back out for *Much Ado About Nothing*, and this time Faith wore it.

"We need a few more people onstage during the party scene," Audrey said. Her red-rimmed eyes hinted at her exhaustion, but she had the air of someone determined to soldier on. She handed elaborately jeweled and feathered masks to Laura and then one to Eileen. "You don't have to do much."

"That's a relief. I'm not a good actress." Eileen slipped the mask over her head and checked her reflection. "Did people actually wear these gaudy things?"

"It will be fun," Laura said. She put on the mask and giggled. "It's ridiculous. But I love it."

"Thank your stars you're not wearing a bird face," Faith said ruefully.

Watson padded into the costume area and did a double take when he saw his mistress.

Faith laughed. "That's my reaction exactly."

"We only include that one for fun," Audrey said. "It's inspired by the plague doctors in medieval times." She pointed to the long, curved beak. "The theory was to keep the germs away from your nose."

Faith turned from side to side, studying the mask. "It would also keep men away, no doubt."

Wolfe entered the room at that moment, and his startled reaction to Faith's appearance made the women laugh.

"Point made," she said, sliding the mask off.

"Phew. Back to normal," Wolfe said with a grin. "I'm here to pick up my costume."

Wolfe was playing Don Pedro, the man who helped one of the couples in the play become engaged. Viola and Griffith were playing

Hero and Claudio. Nell and Corin were to be Beatrice and Benedick, the fun-loving pair who engaged in battles of wits throughout the play.

Eileen took off her mask and helped Wolfe find his costume on the rack. She'd already taken it in so the breeches would fit. The coat had also needed the sleeves lengthened. These alterations had fixed an image of the absent Will in Faith's mind. He had shorter legs and arms and a much more rotund middle than Wolfe.

"As a reminder," Audrey said to Wolfe, "we're only doing one rehearsal today in costume. Then everyone gets the afternoon off."

"To relax?" Laura said. "It must be hard work doing one play after another." She gave Faith a meaningful look.

When the duo had heard about the time off, they'd made plans for later. They were going to visit Shaw's mother in Turners Mills.

"That and other things," Audrey said vaguely. "We all have business to take care of." She glanced at her phone, which she used to keep time. "You'd better go get ready. We're starting in half an hour."

Rehearsal didn't go well, despite the troupe having done the play numerous times.

"Corin," Bates said, a terse tone entering his voice, "concentrate. I'm not getting any authenticity from you."

Corin was supposed to focus on Nell, but he spent the time watching and reacting to Viola.

And today even Viola, the consummate professional, seemed flustered. She kept forgetting her lines. Finally, she burst into tears.

"What is it?" Bates asked her. "This isn't like you."

Viola accepted a handkerchief from Eileen, who was always prepared. "I'm sorry. I keep expecting Sid to walk in."

According to Audrey, the producer had said he might attend rehearsals.

"And it's put you off your game. I can relate to that." Nell pursed her lips, studying her companions. "Our careers are on the line."

Bates paced around the floor in front of the stage. "How about this? I'll ask Sid to give rehearsals a miss for now. But he may want to sit in on one later in the week. On television, there will be lots of rehearsals, and he'll need to see how you handle them."

Faith was relieved that her part consisted of standing onstage and pretending to chatter and laugh with Eileen and Laura. They were merely window dressing, just a level above props.

Although Wolfe suppressed a grin every time he glanced at Faith and her friends.

It happened so often that he finally received a warning from Bates. "Mr. Jaxon, focus on your role, not the lovely ladies in the corner."

Faith bit back a snort at the "lovely ladies" comment.

Wolfe's face reddened, but he didn't argue. "Yes sir." For the rest of the rehearsal, he resolutely kept his gaze off Faith and the others.

Afterward, Faith and Laura grabbed sandwiches and bottles of water and headed out into the cold to Faith's Honda.

"I hope she starts," Faith said. It had been days since she'd driven the SUV.

Laura shivered. "It's freezing out here." Her little face barely showed between her thick pom-pom hat and her scarf, which was wrapped around her chin.

Faith turned the key. The engine cranked a little reluctantly, but then it caught with a roar. She heaved a sigh of relief. "We'll get heat in a minute." After letting the engine warm up, she pulled out of the space and proceeded down the drive.

Laura opened the vents when hot air began to trickle in. "Want me to unwrap your sandwich for you?"

"Sure. That would be great."

Laura pulled their meal out of her tote and handed Faith half a sandwich.

Faith navigated the familiar route to Lighthouse Bay, holding her sandwich in one hand. In town, they stopped to buy a bouquet of flowers.

Then, back in the car, Faith asked, "Which way to Turners Mills?"

"Turn left, then follow that road. It will lead us right there." Laura finished her sandwich. "Water?" She foraged in her tote for two plastic bottles.

Faith took the bottle, uncomfortably reminded of Shaw accepting an open soda from Audrey. "Do you think the soda was poisoned? I can't figure out when someone could have spiked it."

"It was either that or the cookies. But we all ate the cookies."

A thought struck Faith so forcibly she gasped.

Laura shrieked and grabbed the door handle.

"Sorry," Faith said, a little embarrassed. "I just realized something."

Laura released the handle with a laugh. "Warn me next time, okay? What is it?"

"Do you remember what kind of soda Shaw was drinking? I wonder if it was different than the others." She explained to Laura how Shaw had pointed to a specific bottle.

"I don't, but hang on a minute." Laura pulled out her phone. "I'll ask Len. He can check the film for us." She sent him a text.

Faith knew it was a long shot, but the theory tantalized her the rest of the way to Turners Mills. If Shaw preferred a certain drink and it was the only one of that kind, someone could have tampered with it in advance. That meant Griffith or Audrey had to be involved. And what if someone else had grabbed the bottle? It was a risky way to kill someone, for certain.

Mrs. Hastings lived in an attractive ranch home in a neighborhood of similar houses. Feeders near the front picture window were filled with darting, colorful birds.

"My parents live a couple of streets over," Laura said. "This was our neighborhood."

"It's nice," Faith said. She parked behind a small sedan in the driveway. Rather than hop right out, she removed the key from the ignition and sat, butterflies fluttering in her belly. She hated to intrude on a grieving mother.

Laura picked up on her feelings. "I know how you feel. But believe me, we're doing the right thing. Someone needs to find justice for Shaw."

"All right, let's do it." Faith retrieved the bouquet and followed Laura to the door.

Laura rang the bell.

After a minute, a woman in her midthirties answered. Her face crumpled, and she burst into tears. "Laura, it's so good to see you." She gave the visitor a hug.

After a prolonged greeting, Laura told Faith, "This is Sadie, Shaw's sister."

Sadie cuffed Laura on the arm. "I used to babysit this scamp."

Faith introduced herself and handed Sadie the flowers. "I'm so sorry to meet you under these circumstances," she murmured.

"Thank you." Sadie buried her nose in the flowers. "These are lovely. Come on in. Mom will be glad to see you." She showed them to the living room, where Mrs. Hastings sat in a recliner, watching the birds.

To Faith's dismay, she noticed the woman didn't look well. She was thin and frail with a sallow complexion, and there was an oxygen tank placed nearby.

"You remember Laura, don't you, Mom?" Sadie asked. "This is her friend Faith. They've come to visit with you. See these lovely flowers they brought?" She set them on the end table next to her mother's chair.

Mrs. Hastings pulled her attention from the birds playing outside the window and gazed at the bouquet.

Sadie moved to the doorway. "Excuse me while I put on coffee."

Mrs. Hastings gave Laura a wan smile. "You're all grown up. Aren't you lovely?" She turned to Faith. "Nice to meet you."

Again, Faith extended her condolences. She and Laura perched on the sofa, which was so soft that sitting on the edge was probably the only way to keep from being engulfed by it.

Laura and Mrs. Hastings made small talk about Laura's parents, the neighborhood, and Laura's college courses. Faith could tell Laura was avoiding the topics of Shaw and Castleton Manor for now.

Sadie returned with a tray of coffee and oatmeal cookies. She dispensed mugs of coffee and passed around the cookies, then sat in an armchair beside her mother.

Mrs. Hastings broke a cookie in half and took a bite. "Laura, Shaw always thought the world of you."

Her gentle words made Laura break down. "I really cared about him too." She used her napkin to wipe her eyes. "That's why Faith and I are going to figure out who killed him."

Faith sucked in a breath, taken aback by Laura's bold claim. "We're going to try, anyway," she temporized. "Of course we won't interfere with the police investigation."

"Of course," Laura echoed. "But there aren't many clues, and being questioned by the police tends to make people clam up."

"I can understand that," Sadie said. "I get nervous whenever I see blue lights in my rearview mirror, even if I'm not speeding."

Mrs. Hastings studied Faith as if she were probing her intentions. "I think I've heard about you. You've solved quite a few mysteries, haven't you?" She cracked a lopsided smile. "The crime-solving librarian."

Faith's skin heated, and she shifted on her sofa cushion, which nearly swallowed her. "Yes, although I never seek them out. I somehow find myself in the middle of situations." After fighting her way back to an upright position, she said, "I was there when Shaw was stricken. I want to bring whoever hurt him to justice."

"Oh, my poor Shaw." Mrs. Hastings leaned back in her chair and stared up at the ceiling. "He never was able to get ahead in life, ever since—"

Sadie reached a hand out to comfort her mother. "You don't have to talk about it if it upsets you."

Faith guessed they were referring to Shaw's brush with the law when he was younger.

Laura winced. "I hate to say it, but I think it might have something to do with what happened. A lot of people from back then are at the manor right now."

"Seriously?" Sadie raised her brows. "Who and why?"

"We're hosting a Shakespeare week, and I understand several of the actors come from Turners Mills," Faith explained.

"Griffith, Corin, and Audrey," Laura said. "Oh, and Len too. They all joined the same theater company under Bates Beaumont."

"Bates Beaumont," Mrs. Hastings mused. "I remember reading about him in a magazine. He had a wife who vanished, right? And a daughter who has... problems." She tsked. "Goes to show you, people in every walk of life have heartache."

There was truth in those words, Faith reflected. She picked at a cookie, waiting for Laura and the other women to lead the discussion of such sensitive topics.

"Shaw was friends with all those kids," Mrs. Hastings said. "They grew up in this neighborhood."

"I remember them all right." Sadie's lips twisted with distaste. "They were like a feral pack running around the streets. I'm not surprised they became actors. They all had huge egos. Except Len. He was almost normal."

Faith and Laura exchanged looks at Sadie's bitterness.

"Well, to be fair, Audrey doesn't act," Laura said. "She's a stage manager."

"That's because she flopped in that high school play," Sadie responded. "Rather than try harder, she gave up."

"Don't be so hard on them," Mrs. Hastings said. "They were only kids."

Sadie grunted. "I'm sorry. I believed Shaw when he said he was framed. One of them bullied that old man. And it wasn't Shaw."

Faith took a sip of coffee, which made her remember the wild idea she'd formulated on the drive over. "This may sound like an odd question, but did Shaw have a favorite soft drink?"

"That is weird," Sadie said bluntly. "What's that got to do with anything?"

"In a case like this," Faith replied, "we're searching for any clues that could explain what happened. We can't figure out how he got the tainted bottle of soda or when it was tampered with."

"He liked root beer," his mother said. She coughed, putting a hand to her mouth.

Sadie regarded her mother with concern.

Mrs. Hastings waved her daughter off. "Especially when you dropped a scoop of vanilla ice cream in it. It was his favorite treat."

Laura's phone dinged. She held it up. "Bingo. Len said that's what Shaw was drinking."

Confirmation they were on the right track. Now they had to find out if the killer knew root beer was Shaw's favorite or if it was merely a coincidence. That might tell them when the poison was added to the drink.

Mrs. Hastings began to cough more violently.

This time, Sadie got up to assist her mother. "I'm sorry," she said over her shoulder, "but you'll need to excuse us. Thanks for trying to help. We appreciate it."

Faith and Laura made a hasty exit.

"I hope we didn't upset Mrs. Hastings too much," Faith said once they closed the front door behind them. "I feel terrible."

Laura pressed her lips together. "I'm sure the whole situation is taking quite a toll. We were just the frosting on the cake."

That wasn't very comforting, but Faith didn't press the issue. Instead, as she got into the car and started the engine, she hoped they could solve the mystery of Shaw's death. Perhaps that would give his grieving mother a measure of comfort. At least they'd learned a couple of interesting pieces of information. Shaw had been accused of bullying an old man, and he favored root beer.

They arrived back at the manor with time to spare before dinner.

"I'm going upstairs for a while," Faith said as they entered the deserted lobby. She rarely got a break during event weeks, and she planned to make the most of this one. The idea of a hot bath and a book sounded wonderful about now.

"Me too," Laura said. "I've got a school paper to work on."

Upstairs, the hallways were equally hushed.

They had just reached the door of their suite when a piercing scream rang out.

10

Faith dropped the room key in surprise.

The scream continued, rising in intensity.

"It sounds like it's coming from Audrey's room." Laura bolted farther down the hall.

After Faith snatched up the key and threw it back into her bag, she rushed to follow.

Laura knocked on the partially open door, then pushed it open without waiting for a response. "What's going on?"

Faith and Laura cautiously entered the suite.

Audrey stood in the middle of the room, pointing at something with a shaking hand. But at least she had stopped screaming.

Several cushions had been arranged on a chair to resemble a body. On top of the cushions rested a skull. But while that was disturbing enough, the handwritten message in bold red lettering that was propped on his "chest" was even worse.

I know what you did.

Laura put her arm around Audrey. "It's only Yorick. Come sit down." She led the frightened woman to the settee beside the fireplace.

"What does this mean?" Faith asked, studying the sign.

Audrey put a hand over her mouth and shook her head.

Laura draped a blanket over Audrey's shoulders. "Shall I ring for a hot drink?"

Before Audrey could answer, Corin burst through the door. His hair was rumpled, and his cheek had a crease, obvious signs that he'd been napping. "What's going on in here? Someone was screaming fit to wake the dead."

"She came in and saw that," Faith said, motioning to the skull. "It startled her."

"'I know what you did.' Hmm." Corin cocked his head. "What did you do, Audrey? I'd really like to know."

Audrey buried her face in her hands and refused to answer.

Laura glared at him. "Go away. You're making things worse."

He laughed in response and sauntered farther into the room.

"What's all this?" Nell popped through the door. Dressed in a bathrobe and slippers, she had a towel wrapped around her head. "I thought someone was being murdered in here." She clapped a hand over her mouth at her tactless remark. "Oops."

No one responded.

Squinting at the sign, Nell shuffled over to the chair. She reached out a hand. "Ooh, someone's been naughty."

"Stop. Don't touch it," Laura barked. "It's evidence."

Nell raised her eyebrows. "Evidence of what? Surely it's only a joke."

Corin lounged against the mantel, staring down at Audrey. "Maybe, maybe not." He smirked. "We all have secrets, don't we?"

Again, Audrey didn't answer. She hunched her shoulders, leaning over as if trying to disappear.

Laura patted her shoulder, casting a worried glance at Faith.

Faith thought of a way to get rid of Corin and Nell. She pulled her cell phone out of her bag. "I'm giving the police a call. They'll want to see this." She smiled at them. "And you two can be witnesses."

As she hoped, the two actors rushed toward the door at the magic word *police*.

"Not me," Corin said, lifting his hands. "I did nothing, and I know nothing." He slipped out the door and into the hall.

When Nell followed him, their laughter and whispers filtered back into the room.

"It's not funny!" Laura yelled into the hallway, her face thunderous.

"I'm not quite convinced of their innocence." Faith gave a start. Had she actually said that out loud? She always tried to be discreet since accusing people without evidence often backfired, especially when they were important guests at the manor. All she needed was for someone to run to Marlene and complain. She suppressed that thought with a shiver.

"I have no doubts Corin and Nell did it," Laura announced. She folded her arms across her chest. "Are you going to call the police?"

Faith glanced down, realizing she was still holding her phone. She swiped the screen to bring up the dial pad. "Yes, I am."

"Please don't," Audrey said. "I'm sure it was only a prank." She straightened her shoulders. "You don't know this gang like I do. They push everything to the limit, and if you react, then you lose." Her smile was bleak. "I guess I'm the loser today."

Faith and Laura exchanged dubious looks.

Audrey's words only confirmed to Faith that Nell and Corin probably were responsible. Considering that a young man had died recently, it was in very poor taste. Were they implying that Audrey had killed him? Or did the note refer to another incident? Or was Audrey right and it meant nothing at all?

"If you're sure." Faith snapped a couple of pictures of Yorick and his message. "But let's keep the sign just in case."

"Why?" Audrey sounded confused. She got up and began to dismantle the dummy, setting the skull gently aside.

Faith inhaled, then released a long breath. "What if it isn't a joke?"

"That's right," Laura chimed in. "Maybe it's a warning. Shaw was murdered. What if someone thinks you—"

"What? That I killed him?" Audrey's laugh was dry. "Well, I didn't. As for anything else, that was ages ago." She fluffed up the pillows and tossed them onto her bed, where they'd come from. "We all need to move on, right?"

Laura huffed. "I didn't mean that. What if you know something, and the killer doesn't want you to come forward?"

Audrey snorted. "I don't know anything. All I did was hand Shaw a bottle of soda."

Faith wasn't assuming Audrey's guilt or innocence. But she did think of something she wanted to know. "This may sound like a strange question." She seemed to have a bad habit of asking those, she realized. "But was Shaw's soda sealed when you twisted off the lid?"

It took a moment before understanding dawned in Audrey's eyes. "I'm not sure. But I do remember it was easier to open than the other bottles."

A tingling sensation in her hands and arms told Faith that this was an important clue. Unfortunately it didn't reveal the real mystery.

Who had poisoned Shaw?

The cat trotted down the path, moving quickly so his pads wouldn't freeze. While he enjoyed playing in the fluffy white snow sometimes, winter was not his favorite season. It often brought back memories of how he'd been homeless and hungry until his dear human came along.

To take his mind off these unpleasant thoughts, he focused on tracking his prey. The tall, red-haired human was trudging down to the docks, dressed in her very odd attire. The black, rubbery coating reminded him of the seals that swam in the bay. To entertain himself, since most of his friends were hibernating, he imagined that she was one of them.

As they moved in tandem down the snowy path, he managed to close the distance between them without her noticing. She seemed to be heading for the boathouse, where he'd nearly drowned once, but he needed to know what she was up to.

Down at the boathouse, the red-haired woman hailed the man in charge of the boats. He was clearing snow off the dock. "Glenn, I'm glad I caught you."

The man—with long black whiskers that the cat envied—stopped to rest on his snow shovel. He gestured at the small canvas-covered sailboat moored along the dock. "I've been keeping an eye on your boat as you asked."

"Thanks."

"What can I do for you, Miss Beaumont?"

The woman rubbed her mouth with her glove. "Do you have much knowledge of the waters around here?" she asked, sounding distracted.

The dockmaster grinned. "Knowledge? I know 'em like the back of my hand." He gazed out over the stormy gray water reflecting the twilight sky, edged by a band of yellow that foretold more bad weather. "I grew up in Lighthouse Bay, and my earliest memories are of 'messing about in boats,' as they say."

The cat pricked up his ears. He'd heard his human say that very thing. It was from one of those objects she adored—almost as much as him—called a book.

The redhead laughed. "Mine too. Anyway, I'm trying to find out about islands with natural harbors around here." She laughed again. "Just in case I need to head for shore in a hurry."

The man glanced out to sea as though he could view the islands from here. "Let's take a gander at the charts, and I'll mark them for you." He shook his head. "I don't understand why you want to venture out there in this weather. But if you do, I'll make sure you're safe."

"Thank you. That is so kind."

The woman's attention was elsewhere, so the cat made his move. Crouching low, he pounced, leaping with graceful length to land on the woman's foot. Bull's-eye!

She screamed in shock, then relaxed when she saw it was only a cat. "What are you doing, you naughty creature?" She lifted her foot and nudged him off. "Don't you dare claw my suit. If it's full of holes, it won't keep me warm."

The cat wondered if that was also true of seals. Too bad he couldn't get close enough to find out. But that would be mean, he decided. And he was a nice cat.

Backstage was bedlam the next evening. Not only was Sid Meyers attending the performance of *Much Ado About Nothing*, but he had convinced Wolfe and Bates to let him film the performance. "Shakespeare, live from Castleton Manor," he gushed. "Can't you just see it?"

Sid had waxed poetic about the gorgeous Great Hall Gallery and its candlelit ambience. Those wearing costumes would be offered front-row seats to give the setting a historic feel. "Like we've traveled back in time to the Globe," he said. "I can't turn down this opportunity."

"At least we don't have to worry about payroll this week," Griffith said as he grabbed the pointed shoes and hat that went with his Claudio costume. "I heard Sid is paying Bates a pretty penny for filming us."

This statement struck Faith, who was helping Eileen with costumes. A man who owned a book worth millions of dollars was worried about money? Perhaps it was all tied up in that book and other possessions. She could understand Bates not wanting to part with the incredible *First Folio*. It was an irreplaceable treasure.

Viola ran up, carrying the gold-and-salmon brocade dress she wore as Hero, the woman in love with Claudio. "Look what happened." She displayed the dress, which had a huge gash down the back. Tears sprang to her eyes. "Who could have done this?"

Faith glanced at the other actors, who were busy with their own affairs. She examined the tear. It appeared to have been made with a knife, instead of a rip along the seam. "Eileen, do you think you can fix it?"

Eileen was sewing a button on a coat. She set it aside and came up beside Faith. "Let me see." Inspecting the gown closely, she ran her fingers over the fabric. "I certainly can. Give me a few minutes." She placed the garment over the arm of her chair and foraged for the right color thread in the basket.

Viola plopped into a chair and sighed. "I suppose I shouldn't be surprised. The pranks were bound to target me sooner or later."

Slicing a costume right before a performance was a pretty severe prank. Faith thought it was more in the realm of vandalism than mischief. She picked up the bird mask, thankful now that she'd be wearing it. She wasn't really excited about appearing on television.

"What's going on, Viola?" Griffith asked, looming over the diminutive actress in her chair. "A touch of stage fright?"

"Hardly," Corin said as he joined them. "Viola's far too experienced of an actress to let a camera scare her."

Viola studied the two men vying for her attention. "I'm fine about the filming. But not so happy that someone is trying to sabotage me." Her clear voice rang out like a bell.

Faith noticed Nell duck out of view behind the rack of clothing. Was she the culprit?

Griffith rested his hands on his hips, frowning. His feathered hat sat cockeyed on his head. "Who would do that? You're the star."

"Exactly." Viola's smile brought to mind a kitten enjoying cream. "But it's not going to work. All the tricks in the world won't dampen my talent." She rose from the chair and turned to Eileen. "Please have someone bring the dress to me. I'll be in the dressing room doing my makeup. Thank you." She pushed past the two men, who stared after her.

Perdita had entered the room, and she paused to watch Viola saunter away, her pert nose in the air. "Guess it's true what they say. You need an ironclad ego to succeed in this business." With a shake of her flowing hair, she turned to Faith. "I'm going to join the cast tonight. Can you help me find something to wear?"

Viola had stopped near the rack where Nell was lurking. "How do you know when you're the best?" she announced in ringing tones. "When other people try to bring you down."

The room fell silent.

"Are you accusing me of something?" Nell pranced out into the open. "You'd better mind your p's and q's."

Audrey ran into the room. "Has anyone seen the scroll? It's missing."

Perdita tilted her head, eyeing Audrey suspiciously. "He should have hired me," she muttered under her breath.

Audrey huffed at Perdita but said nothing.

"Can you imagine?" Griffith said to Corin. "Audrey has lost something. Again."

The other actor twirled his finger near his temple. "Like her mind?"

Viola spared Audrey a glance, then returned her gaze to Nell. "Face it. You've been jealous of me since day one."

Nell scoffed. "Me, jealous of the likes of you? I'm carrying these plays with my wit and timing."

"Ladies," Audrey snapped at the quarreling actresses, "we're on in fifteen. Get on with your business."

The rivals ignored her and continued to squabble.

Faith helped Perdita cobble together a costume while Audrey tore apart the props area searching for the scroll. The uproar had reached fever pitch when a piercing whistle cut through like a knife.

Once again the room fell silent.

Wolfe held up the missing scroll. "I found this taped to Agatha Christie's hand." He referred to the statue in the Great Hall Gallery.

"Oh, thank you." Audrey accepted the prop from him.

"Pipe down, all of you," Wolfe continued. "I could hear the commotion from the other room, which is extremely unprofessional. Ten minutes to curtain, and if you're not dressed and ready, we'll have to cancel. It'd be a shame to send those cameras away." His innate authority, tempered with his usual charm, had the desired effect.

A few minutes later, Laura, dressed in her costume, strode into the room. She shook her ringlets—created with Faith's curling iron—and asked, "What did I miss?"

Faith caught Eileen's eye, and the two of them laughed.

"The short answer is, 'total chaos,'" Faith said. "Let's put on our masks, ladies."

Despite the rocky start, the play went well. Faith discovered that she enjoyed her role as lady-in-waiting. Thanks to the mask covering her face, she found herself surprisingly unselfconscious while she moved about the stage, almost forgetting the camera watching like an unblinking eye. At the same time she noticed how the knowledge of being filmed spurred the actors to new heights of talent and showmanship. Even Wolfe exhibited a fine polish.

"Are you staying for the cast party?" Faith asked Eileen after the curtain.

Her aunt considered. "I suppose I could for a while." She grinned. "I had a blast."

They headed for Faith's suite to change out of their costumes.

"I'm so envious you're staying here," Eileen said as they padded along the dense carpet. "What a treat."

"It sure has been." *For the most part*, Faith reflected. She could do without the murder and mayhem, though.

Perdita thundered down the hall, her eyes wide with panic, dropping papers as she went. Oddly she was wearing a long black robe over her costume. "Help! Help! Audrey is ill."

The woman's squawking cries, along with her strange attire, put Faith in mind of flapping crows and portents of doom. Then she realized what Perdita was saying. "What's wrong with Audrey?"

Perdita halted, breathing heavily. She waved the papers she held. "I came up to give her some of my notes, but when I got there, she was passed out." She sucked in another breath. "She won't wake up."

"Uh-oh," Eileen muttered. "That doesn't sound good." She eyed Perdita up and down and sent Faith a confused look.

Faith used her brows to indicate she'd fill her in later concerning the decidedly odd young woman. "Let's go check on Audrey," she said to Perdita.

Without a word, Perdita whirled around and led the way, garments billowing.

Faith and Eileen followed her.

What struck Faith when they entered the room was the sense that the scene had been staged. Lit candles flickered around the otherwise dark room. Audrey lay on the big canopy bed, ankles crossed and arms flung wide. An empty glass rested on the floor.

As Faith crept closer, she saw ripped pieces of paper lying beside Audrey. On the bedside table were evergreen needles and a few red berries.

A knot of cold shock settled in Faith's stomach. She quickly crossed the rest of the way to the bed and picked up Audrey's hand.

She couldn't feel a pulse.

"Call 911," Faith heard herself say as if from a great distance. "I think she's dead."

11

Faith gently set Audrey's hand on the cotton sheet, her shock deepening into dread and sorrow. To distract her mind, Faith tried to block out Perdita's shrieks and her own emotions and focus on the scene. Once the police arrived, she wouldn't have another chance to search for clues as to what had happened.

While Eileen called for help, Faith pulled out her phone and quickly took shots of the evergreens and the pieces of paper. Only one displayed a complete sentence: *I have always loved you.* The rest were so finely torn they contained only single words or letters.

"What are you doing?" Perdita asked. She took a giant step closer. "Are you some kind of ghoul?"

Faith thought about asking Perdita the same thing, considering her dark attire and peculiar behavior, but she managed to hold her tongue.

Even stranger, for the second time within the week, this volatile young woman was first to find a recently deceased person. Was she responsible for their deaths? For Shaw, Faith didn't know a motive, but according to her own father, Perdita had wanted Audrey's job. *Badly enough to kill for it?*

Perdita reached the foot of the bed. "Do you think she killed herself? Maybe that paper is a ripped-up suicide note."

Faith couldn't say for sure. "Don't touch anything," she warned. "It's a crime scene now."

"They'll be here in a few minutes," Eileen said. She huddled by the doorway, distress and fear creasing her face. "Should we stay in here or go out into the hall?"

"I think out in the hall," Faith answered. "We've probably contaminated the scene already."

Then Faith glimpsed one last item of interest on the floor, a book on herbal poisons wrapped in a plastic library binding. Suppressing a snort of disbelief, she used a tissue to open the book. The ink stamp inside revealed that it came from the library in Turners Mills. Had Audrey actually checked out the damning book, or had someone planted it in her room?

"I thought you weren't supposed to touch anything," Perdita snapped.

Faith released the cover and waved the tissue. "I used this. And I touched the book where most people don't." She had used the bottom corner, since most people grabbed the center of the cover when opening a book.

After scanning the room one last time, Faith ushered the other two out into the hall.

"I hope they don't take long," Eileen said, putting a hand to her midriff. Her face had taken on a greenish hue.

Concerned, Faith steered her aunt to a side chair placed along the wall. "Do you want a drink of water?"

Before Eileen could answer, Perdita began striding down the hall. "I'm going to tell the others what happened."

Eileen looked up at Faith. "Go with her. I'll be all right."

"Are you sure?" Faith was torn between assisting Eileen and being there when the rest of the troupe learned about Audrey's death. Their unguarded reactions, especially among a group of actors, could be critical to finding out what had happened.

Her aunt's nod was decisive. "Go on. Quickly. She's already at the staircase."

Faith trotted after Perdita, finally breaking into an outright run to catch her. The pair raced down the main staircase and toward the billiard room, the troupe's usual gathering place.

On Perdita's heels, Faith heard Griffith's exclamation when Perdita flew into the room. "What are you? The harbinger of doom?"

The other actors stopped talking to listen to the answer.

Perdita lifted her chin, straightening to her full height. "You might say that. Audrey is dead."

Her bald announcement was met with stunned silence, although someone gasped.

Then reactions hit, rippling through the crowd like a wave. Corin groaned and sank into the closest chair. Griffith bent over and cradled his face in his hands. Viola dropped her cue stick, and it rolled under the table. Len leaped to retrieve it. Nell screwed up her face into a grimace.

Bates hurried forward, and for the first time, Faith noticed the director and his producer friend, Sid Meyers.

"What are you talking about?" Bates appeared troubled as he studied his daughter's face.

"I'm not imagining things." Perdita's tone was both ironic and offended. "Ask Faith."

Wincing, Faith stepped farther into the room. "It's true. Perdita told my aunt and me that something was wrong with Audrey. When we went to check on her, we found her lying on her bed, unresponsive." She bit her lip, feeling the telltale tremble of tears brewing.

"The police are coming," Perdita said. Spreading her wide sleeves in a dramatic gesture, she intoned, "They'll figure out if it was suicide or murder."

Sid, who had been watching in silence, set down his glass. "I think that's my cue, Bates. I'll head back to the city and let you take care of business."

"You can't go," Perdita objected. "They'll want to talk to you." She stabbed a finger at each person. "All of you."

"But I don't even know the woman," Sid said. "So there is no reason to hold me."

"Perdita," Bates hissed. He had the haunted, desperate expression of a man who was watching his life implode before his very eyes. "I'm sorry, Sid. We're all upset by this tragedy. I'm sure the police will let you leave." He turned to Faith, his eyes pleading. "When are they coming?"

"Any minute," Faith said. "They're usually quite fast to respond."

Sid worked his way through the crowd and pressed a business card into Faith's limp fingers. "Tell them to call me if they need to." He faced the troupe. "Goodbye, all. Nice job tonight. Bates, we'll talk."

Corin ran after Sid. "Wait. I'll walk you out."

"Trust Corin to seize the moment," Nell said. "Unreal." Her pout implied that she wished she'd thought of it first.

Faith decided it was time to excuse herself. "Now that you all know about poor Audrey, I'm going to go back upstairs and wait with my aunt. She's been holding vigil." She thought of something. "Has anyone seen Laura?"

Headshakes and denials met her inquiry.

Where could she be? Faith hadn't seen Laura since the play had ended. Out in the hallway, she met Brooke, who was pushing a cart full of sandwiches and cookies toward the party.

She smiled when she saw Faith. "Hello, stranger. Great job tonight."

The performance now seemed like ages ago. "Thanks. It was fun. Have you seen Laura, by any chance?"

Brooke frowned. "She's not in the billiard room? Last time I saw her was after the play. She said she was going upstairs to change."

Faith's heart lurched. "Well, I can't imagine where she is." She hesitated, not wanting to disrupt Brooke's happy mood, then decided it was better for her to hear bad news from a friend. "Something awful happened tonight." She told her about Audrey and mentioned that she was headed back up to wait with Eileen.

Brooke gasped. "That's awful. I'm so sorry to hear it." She glanced both ways down the quiet corridor. "Listen, let me deliver this food to the famished horde, and then I'll join you. I'm basically off the clock as of right now."

"Great." Faith was already moving away. "And I'm going to look for Laura." Fear lent her feet wings as she ran up the stairs. She prayed the college student was all right. Of course Faith had never even made it into the Shakespeare suite. Maybe Laura was there, already in bed or relaxing.

Right. As if Laura would miss the staff party. She had been flying high with adrenaline after the curtain call.

Watson met Faith at the top of the stairs with a plaintive mew.

"What is it, Rumpy? I don't have time right now."

In answer, he wound around her legs, then raced down the hallway in the opposite direction.

"Where are you going?"

He stopped and meowed again.

Faith knew from experience that he wouldn't relent until she followed. She sighed. "Make it fast. I'm on a mission here."

The cat's long stare seemed to say, "So am I." He darted down the corridor.

This wing wasn't in use at the moment, so the hallway was dimly lit. As Faith padded along the carpet, she noticed how quiet it was. If not for Watson, she would have been entirely alone.

Not quite. Watson had run ahead and was standing beside a window seat in a little alcove. Lying on the cushion was a familiar figure.

Laura.

Her heart in her throat, Faith ran to Laura's side, kicking aside a pile of brown fur. The bear costume, she realized. In a ghastly repeat of the scene only minutes before with Audrey, she felt for a pulse.

This time she was rewarded with the steady beat under the young woman's pale skin. She shook her shoulder gently. "Laura, wake up."

To her great relief, Laura's eyelashes fluttered. She blinked. "Faith?" Then she winced and reached for the back of her head. "I have a really bad headache." She started to sit up.

But Faith pressed down on her shoulders. "Don't get up. I'm going to find someone to check you over." She stepped back and tripped over the bear costume. She picked it up, planning to move it out of the way. "Why is this here?"

"I have no idea." Laura frowned at the bundle of brown fur. "I think I saw someone wearing it, though." She squinted. "I *think*. Everything is fuzzy. Viola. I did see Viola."

All that was intriguing, but Faith had to take care of business first. She dumped the pile of fabric onto a chair, then spotted the head on the floor and set it on top. "Don't try to talk. I'll be right back." She hurried down the hallway.

Watson remained at Laura's side, keeping her company until help arrived.

Chief Garris was emerging from the elevator, Officer Laddy a pace behind him. "Faith, I understand there's been another death?"

"Yes, but before we get to that, did the paramedics arrive?"

"They're here already," Laddy said. "It's protocol to have them on-site."

Faith pointed. "I found Laura lying unconscious on a window seat down there. I think she might have been hit on the head. She's awake now, but I think she should be examined."

"I'll go get someone ASAP, Chief," Laddy said, then rushed away.

Faith and the chief continued to Audrey's room.

"I understand Eileen called 911," Garris said.

"Yes, she did. She and I were on the way to my room when Perdita Beaumont raised the alarm about Audrey." Faith gave him a bare outline of the situation. "We did our best not to disturb anything once we realized she was dead." But she couldn't resist adding, "I did see evergreen needles on her nightstand. I wonder if it's yew."

Garris didn't comment, but Faith sensed his gears turning.

A door opened to Faith's right, releasing the soaring strains of baroque classical music.

"What's going on out here?" Marlene peeked out of the room, a towel wrapped around her head and a green clay mask adorning her features. No doubt due to the mask's stiffness, she wasn't wearing her usual frown of disapproval.

An EMT and Laddy approached.

"Where's the patient?" the EMT asked.

Faith recognized the stocky, kind young man as one of the workers who had attended Shaw. "I'll show you," she said, glad to leave Garris to deal with Marlene.

Watson was still by Laura's side when they got there.

The EMT examined Laura. Thankfully, he said she was going to be fine, but he warned her about watching for signs of a concussion and urged her to visit her doctor the next morning, even if she felt okay. Since the bump was on the back of her head and she had been found lying faceup, it was obvious she had been hit on the head and then moved.

"You'll have to take a couple of days off," Faith said.

"But I can't skip work," Laura protested. She sat up on the window seat, with Watson purring in her lap. "I need to—"

"It's all right," Faith interrupted. "I'll clear it with Marlene."

The paramedic turned to Officer Laddy. "If we're all done here, I'll go back to the other case."

"Other case?" Laura asked, glancing between Faith and the police officer. "What are you talking about?"

"She doesn't know?" Laddy asked Faith.

"I haven't had a chance to tell her," Faith replied. She turned to Laura and spoke softly to blunt the impact of her words. "Audrey is dead. The police are here to investigate."

Laura gasped. "Audrey?" She covered her mouth with one hand.

Faith nodded and sat beside Laura on the window seat and took her hand. "Why don't you tell Officer Laddy what you saw before someone hit you?"

Laddy whipped out his phone, shifting into detective gear. "Yes, please do. Since you were attacked, I need to take a statement." He started taking notes. "Any idea what happened?"

Laura shook her head. "I was walking along the hall to our room after the play. I thought I heard someone behind me. The next thing I knew, Faith was leaning over me."

"So you weren't in this vicinity when you were attacked?" Laddy asked.

"Our room is in the other corridor," Laura said. "Near Audrey's." Her mouth trembled, and she blinked back tears. "What happened to her?"

Faith squeezed her friend's hand. "First tell him about the bear costume and Viola," she prompted. She believed that anything Laura witnessed in the hallway might have a bearing on both incidents.

Laura scratched Watson under his chin, her unseeing gaze focused on the carpet. "Let's see. After the play ended, I came upstairs to change. Faith, you and Eileen were still downstairs talking to people." She took a breath. "At the top of the stairs, I thought I saw someone in the bear costume."

The officer's busy fingers hitched. "Bear costume?"

Faith slid out of the window seat and picked up the fur outfit, head in one hand, body in the other. "This is one of the costumes. People have been having fun wearing it around the manor." She dropped it back into the chair.

"Okay," Laddy said, drawing out the word. "Do you have any idea who was wearing the costume?"

Laura frowned. "I wish I did. I just waved at the bear and kept going."

"After that, did you see anything else?" the officer persisted.

"I saw Viola leave Audrey's room."

12

Laura's announcement sent a wave of shock through Faith.

Judging by Officer Laddy's expression, he was equally galvanized. "You're certain about that?" His voice was almost a bark.

Laura drew back, her eyes wide. "Very certain." Her mouth dropped open. "Do you think—"

"Don't make any assumptions," Laddy warned. "Leave the investigation to us. Tell me exactly what you saw and heard."

Laura explained that she had been almost to her room when she saw Audrey's door open and Viola emerge. The actress passed by with only a nod of greeting and kept going toward the stairs.

"Did she seem upset? Guilty? Furtive?" Laddy asked.

"No, she seemed perfectly cool and calm." Laura shrugged. "But she's an actress, after all."

There was the rub, Faith realized. As the Bard had said, all the world was a stage.

And who better to take advantage of that than a theater troupe?

"I'm glad you could come with me," Faith told Brooke the next day. They were on their way to the library in Turners Mills.

"Me too. I've barely had a minute off since the event started." Brooke studied the passing winter landscape hunkered under iron-gray clouds. "Uh-oh. I think we're going to get that storm they predicted sooner rather than later."

A few flakes twirled down and landed on the windshield. "You're right. Here it comes." Faith hoped they would be able to finish their errand before the snowfall intensified. But she'd been happy to get out of the manor, away from the aura of gloom that had descended after Audrey's death.

"I'm so glad Laura is all right," Brooke said. "I think the killer knocked her out to get her out of the way."

"Me too." Faith had accompanied Laura to the doctor that morning, and she'd been pronounced on the mend. She was now ensconced in the suite with a pile of books and Watson, bundled up beside a roaring fire. Faith had given her orders not to let anyone in, and Brooke had delivered lunch before they left.

The evening before, Chief Garris had interviewed everyone in the troupe as well as the manor employees.

In the discussion among the actors afterward, Faith gathered that Viola was the last person to admit seeing Audrey. She said they'd talked about *Twelfth Night*, the next play, and that was all. Perdita said she found Audrey already stricken.

Faith reckoned there was a good half hour between the two visitors, and so far, neither had been arrested. She couldn't tell if the police were still building a case against one of the women or if they had another suspect in mind.

"Who do you think did it?" Brooke asked. "I'm sitting here going back and forth between Viola and Perdita. But what puzzled me is that neither had a connection to Shaw."

"That we know of," Faith reminded her. One thing she firmly believed was that the deaths of Shaw and Audrey were connected, especially since she guessed the same poison had been used.

They reached the village of Turners Mills, and Faith slowed to search for the street where the library was located.

"There it is." Brooke pointed to a sign. "Even though the killer tried to make it look like suicide, I don't believe it for a second. Do you?"

A couple of the actors had suggested that Audrey killed herself over remorse about giving Shaw the poisoned soda.

"The scene seemed too staged." Faith signaled and turned. "Especially that ripped-up love letter."

Although Faith hadn't mentioned to the actors what she'd seen in the room, she had confided in Brooke. Surprisingly, Perdita hadn't blabbed. Perhaps Garris had warned her that it might damage the case.

"Do you think the letter was meant for Griffith?" Brooke asked. "I heard through the grapevine they used to date."

Faith slowed, spotting the brick library ahead. "I wondered about that. She was always gazing at him with a forlorn expression."

"And he's been chasing Viola full tilt. Poor Audrey." Brooke shuddered. "I'd hate to watch my ex go after someone new."

"Me too." Faith had coped with heartbreak by moving from Boston to Lighthouse Bay. At first, even that distance hadn't seemed far enough.

There was a vacant spot between two salt-encrusted sedans, so Faith pulled in and parked.

Faith loved visiting libraries of all types, and this small but beautiful one was delightful. She and Brooke stepped into a marble-floored lobby adorned with tall wood columns. Straight ahead was the main desk, and to each side, rooms lit by stained glass windows beckoned. At this time of day, it was quiet, with only one patron sitting in the reading room.

The older woman behind the desk smiled at them. "Good morning. How may I help you?" She adjusted her glasses, as though taking a better look at the visitors.

Faith approached the desk, returning the woman's smile. "Hi, I'm Faith Newberry, Castleton Manor's librarian, and this is Brooke Milner, chef." She noticed the name plaque on the desk. "Are you Mrs. Brown?"

"Please call me Muriel. The collection at Castleton Manor is simply spectacular. As is the room." She laughed. "Our little library certainly can't compete." She smiled at Brooke. "And I've heard the food is scrumptious."

"You must come to one of our events and see for yourself," Brooke said. "Many are open to the public."

Muriel pointed to an Everything Shakespeare event poster taped to the front of the desk. "I hope to get to one of those plays," she said. "A couple of local young men are acting in them."

"You should," Faith said. "The event has been fabulous." *Besides the murders, that is.*

"So what can I help you with?" Muriel asked.

"I called earlier about picking up some books for Laura Kettrick, another Castleton employee," Faith replied.

Muriel nodded. "Laura's a wonderful young woman."

"Like I said on the phone, she's not feeling well, and she needs some books for a college paper." Faith placed the list of books that she and Laura had put together onto the desk.

Muriel reached for the list. "Let me see if these are available." Adjusting her glasses again, she peered at the computer, her fingers flying over the keyboard. "You're in luck. These are all in."

Even the plant poison book? Faith had included the volume in hopes of learning even a tidbit of information. Muriel couldn't release the name of the borrower, since that was against library regulations.

But now it appeared there hadn't been one.

The cat snuggled closer to his human's friend on the chaise longue. He'd been told to keep an eye on her, and he had every intention of doing a good job. In addition, he was keeping the two angelfish nearby under his watchful eye. That hadn't been requested, but the cat liked to be thorough.

"You're the sweetest. Do you know that?" The human's voice was full of admiration. "I wish I had a cat just like you."

The cat rolled over and stretched, savoring her compliment. He reached up with his front paws and gently batted at her hand, the better to show his appreciation.

"Ooh. You're frisky." Evading his paws, she picked up a bowl of soup from the tray beside her. She dipped a spoon into the liquid, which smelled enticingly of fish.

He sat up and rudely butted his nose against the bowl, something his human would never allow.

This human only laughed. "Want some haddock chowder?" She scooped a spoonful of broth and fish chunks onto a saucer and set it on the floor.

The cat jumped down, his whiskers twitching with anticipation. As he was about to take his first delectable bite, an eerie wail echoed through the room.

"Oh no. There it is again." The human started crying, then put the blanket over her head and hid.

The noise hurt the cat's ears, and at first he considered hiding under the bed to escape it. But seeing the poor human crying made him angry. He'd stop the sound, whatever it was.

He prowled the perimeter of the room, searching for where the sound was coming from.

Aha. Up on the wall and behind a lamp. He jumped up onto the dresser and pushed the lamp aside. It fell to the floor with a crash.

"What are you doing?" the human asked. "I'm going to be in so much trouble for letting you do that."

The cat didn't care about the lamp. He had found the source of the noise, a circular hole hidden in the busy wallpaper pattern.

The wail came again, but this time when it died away, he had a response.

Mustering every bit of cat power he possessed, he gave his most ferocious hiss, following it with his best yowl. He ended his recital with the hair-raising scream he'd learned from fighting a nasty tom in the dark days before his dear human had adopted him.

Silence. The eerie wail was gone.

The human laughed. "You're amazing. Come on. I think you deserve some more fish for that."

"Can you point us in the right direction?" Brooke asked Muriel. "We've never been here before."

The librarian bustled around the desk. "Oh, I'll help you find them. It's quiet right now." She led the way into the reading room, where shelves of reference books stood along the back wall.

Faith and Brooke followed as Muriel efficiently scanned the volumes, finding the requested books. There was a snag when she reached the last one on the list, the book about plant poisons.

Muriel ran her finger along the titles again, as if hoping to find the missing book. She sighed. "I'm sorry. I can't find it. It's either been shelved wrong or stolen." She pressed her lips together in a firm line, no doubt vexed at having to admit this failing.

"No problem. It happens. We'll locate another copy somewhere else." Faith really wanted to study the book to see if yew was one of the poisons mentioned. She had every confidence it was. Otherwise, why would the killer have left it in Audrey's room?

As they walked back toward the checkout desk, Faith said to Muriel, "You must be proud of Corin and Griffith. They're very talented."

Muriel beamed. "They sure are. I was thrilled when they stopped by a couple of weeks ago with Audrey."

Faith tried to hide her surprise at the mention of Audrey. It was obvious Muriel hadn't heard about her death yet, and Faith didn't want to break the news. She glanced at Brooke, and she could tell that her friend felt the same way.

"They said they wanted to make sure I knew about the plays," Muriel continued. "They even brought the poster and a stack of flyers."

Behind the librarian's back, Brooke wiggled her eyebrows at this clue.

Faith was secretly chagrined. The visit must have been when the book was lifted. Unfortunately, any of the three could have taken it.

When no other questions came to mind, Faith took Laura's library card out of her pocket and handed it to Muriel.

As Muriel placed the card under the scanner, she mused, "Castleton. Wasn't Shaw Hastings working there when he died? What a tragedy."

A librarian who isn't above a bit of gossip.

"He worked for me in the kitchen," Brooke said. "It's a real shame. He was a nice guy."

Muriel scanned the first book. "I knew Shaw all his life. He was a sweet little boy. That's why it was so shocking when he was arrested." She set the book down and picked up another one. "I found it hard to believe he'd cause injury to an elderly man."

That sounds serious. While Faith was weighing possible responses, the library door opened, and a stream of elementary children filed in, chattering in excitement.

"I'll be with you in a minute," Muriel called to the harried teacher. To Faith and Brooke she said, "It's our reading hour. One of my favorite parts of the week."

Faith hefted the stack of books with a groan. The window of opportunity to question Muriel was closed—for now.

"I have good news and bad news," Bates announced later that afternoon.

The cast and crew had gathered in the Great Hall Gallery for a run-through of *Twelfth Night*, which was scheduled to be performed the following day.

"The good news is, Sid said the filming of *Much Ado About Nothing* came out great. But..." Bates hesitated. "He's put discussion of further filming on hold."

"Why? Because we're so scandalous?" Griffith glared at his fellow actors. "Maybe we should become a crime-solving show instead of a Shakespeare troupe."

"That's not fair," Nell said. "Audrey killed herself, didn't she? How is that our fault?" She glanced at Viola. "I'll bet some of us are even relieved about it."

Upon Faith's return from Turners Mills, Wolfe had told her that Garris was keeping Laura's assault and other evidence pointing to murder quiet. As a result, gossip that Audrey and Shaw made a suicide pact was circulating, since the same poison had killed them both. But Faith believed they had been murdered—and that the motive for the crime lay in the past.

Viola flounced in her seat, returning Nell's gaze with a glare. "I say we do an awesome job on the remaining plays. Sid will be begging to work with us."

Bates lowered himself to a seated position on the edge of the stage. "I appreciate that attitude, Viola. Many things are out of our control, but maintaining professional standards is not."

"I've got a friend who works at a hip New York arts magazine," Len chimed in. "I can ask him to cover us."

Everyone stared at him. The technician rarely spoke.

"Thanks. Let's talk about that later," Bates said. "But right now I have another announcement. Faith Newberry has kindly agreed to step in for Audrey. Her loss was quite a blow, and I appreciate Faith's willingness to pinch-hit."

Perdita shot out of her chair. "Seriously?" she shrieked at Bates. "When you know that's all I've wanted to do since you started this little troupe? How could you?" Without waiting for an answer, she spun on her heel and stalked out of the room.

Faith's skin heated. Had she put herself in Perdita's sights? But how could she refuse a request from Wolfe? Faith gave the group a half-hearted wave. "Thanks. I'll do my best to fill Audrey's shoes." *And stay alive while doing so.*

Bates didn't react to his daughter's outburst. Instead, he went over some general direction concerning the play, then had the actors get ready for the rehearsal. He gestured to Faith. "I made a couple of changes to the script. Can you please make copies for the cast?" He handed her a few typed pages.

Eager to prove herself useful, Faith nodded. "I'll have these for you right away." The printer in the library was the closest copier, so she pulled out her keys and walked down the gallery to the door.

The vast room was dim, with not even a fire burning today. Not bothering to switch on the overhead lights, Faith pressed the power button on her printer and waited for it to warm up.

The cases holding rare works had their own lights, and her eye was drawn to the one holding the *First Folio*. Once again she thought what a thrill it must be to own such a priceless book.

Then she noticed something odd. The interior of the case seemed different. Had the book fallen over? Concerned, she hurried to check.

The *Folio* was missing.

13

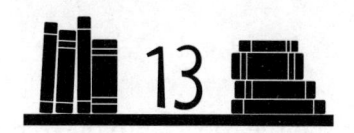

A wave of vertigo washed over Faith, and she had to grab the case to keep from falling. *The* Folio *is gone! Has someone stolen it?*

She staggered to the nearest chair and sat down, groping blindly for the arms to guide her. She lowered her head and breathed deeply, and gradually her panic and breathlessness eased.

The library door opened. "Faith?" Wolfe poked his head around the jamb. "Everything all right in here? You've been gone awhile." When she squeaked in response, he pushed the door open and entered the library. "Is something wrong?"

Faith pointed a shaking finger at the display case. When she could find words, she croaked, "*Folio.* Gone." Behind the panic, a tiny bit of hope fluttered. Maybe Wolfe had moved the book. He had keys as she did. And thankfully her keys had been under her watch all day.

Wolfe moved cautiously toward the case, staring at the shelf where the Shakespeare volume had rested. An expression of concern flashed across his features. Then he relaxed. "Maybe Bates took it. I lent him my keys earlier. He said he wanted to wander around the manor and clear his head."

At his words, all the air left Faith's body. She was light-headed again, this time with relief. But she still needed to put her mind at ease. "Let's ask him. Please?"

"I'll go get him right away." Wolfe pivoted and left the library.

For the first time, Faith noticed he wore a false belly for his role of Sir Toby Belch, and it swung comically when he turned. *He won't need his clothes altered for this role*, she thought, then felt a little guilty.

Faith pushed herself out of the chair and went to the printer, which was ready now. She slid the papers into the feed tray and pushed the button to make copies.

Bates plowed through the library door, with Wolfe behind him. "Wolfe mentioned there's a problem."

Trust Wolfe to be discreet in front of an audience. "I hope not, but there seems to be." Faith pointed to the empty case. "The *Folio* is missing."

"Oh." Bates studied the shelf. "Perdita has it. She wanted to keep a close eye on it, so she removed it from the case and stowed it in her room." His smile was sheepish. "She borrowed the keys you loaned to me, Wolfe." He patted his pocket and removed two small keys. "Here they are."

"Bates." Wolfe's tone was tentative. "I know she's your daughter but . . ." His voice trailed off. For once, the assertive and eloquent businessman appeared at a loss for words.

Faith sent him a silent message of understanding. She was appalled that such a valuable book might be damaged through careless handling. At the same time, the Beaumonts owned the *Folio* and could do whatever they wanted with it. Implying that the unstable Perdita shouldn't have it would be incredibly tactless.

Fortunately, Bates seemed not to notice Wolfe's hesitance. "Now how are those copies coming?" he asked. "We really need them."

"Hey, I thought you two had abandoned me," Laura said, smiling.

When Faith and Brooke entered the suite late that afternoon, they found Laura and Watson curled up where Faith had left them, Laura sipping a cup of tea and reading a book.

"We've been busy," Faith replied. After returning from the library in Turners Mills, Faith and Brooke had gone straight to the cast meeting and the kitchen, respectively.

Laura placed a bookmark in the crease of the book and closed it. "Watson is good company."

The cat purred.

"Are you feeling better?" Faith studied Laura as she set the bag of requested books beside the chaise longue. Laura's color was good and her demeanor chipper. "You look like you are."

"My headache is gone." Laura rubbed the back of her head gently. "And the bump is going down." She smiled. "Guess what Watson did?" She waited a beat. "He scared away the ghost."

Faith plopped down on her bed. This was worth listening to. "What do you mean?" She sent an amused glance at Brooke, who was fussing over her angelfish.

"The ghost. You know, that creepy sound I keep hearing. You heard it too."

That was true, but Faith believed it was merely building noises of some sort. "Tell us what happened."

"While I was eating lunch, the spooky sound started up again. Watson found a speaking tube in the wall, and he hissed and screamed into it. He sounded scary, like a lion or a tiger." Laura gave a mock shiver. "I was almost frightened myself."

Watson raised his head in acknowledgment of being discussed. To Faith's eyes, there was something proud and regal in the set of his features.

"So then what happened?" Brooke asked. She picked up the container of fish food and sprinkled some in the bowl. "Did the ghost go away?"

Laura's smile was triumphant. "It sure did. I haven't heard it since."

Faith went to the wall and examined the brass fitting. She recognized it as an old-fashioned speaking tube used to communicate with servants and between rooms. Had someone been using it to terrorize them? Or maybe it was one of the troupe's pranks. She could imagine Nell pretending to be the ghost from *Hamlet*.

"I'll mention it to Wolfe. At least if it happens again, you know what to do." Faith swooped down and gave Watson a pat. "You're the best, Rumpy."

He pushed against her hand as if to let her know he agreed.

"Did you have any luck at the Turners Mills library?" Laura asked as she unpacked the books. "Besides finding these. Thanks so much."

Brooke settled in a chair by the fire. "We found out that Corin, Griffith, and Audrey visited the library recently. They dropped off a poster and flyers, and we think one of them stole a book."

"The book in Audrey's room wasn't checked out," Faith said. "Muriel also told us a little more about Shaw's problems. She said he hurt an older man."

Laura tapped a hand against her mouth. "She knows more than I do. Many details of the whole situation were hushed up at the time. But I know someone we need to talk to. Griffith."

Downstairs, Faith and Laura intercepted Griffith in the hallway.

The actor was dressed in sweats and carrying a duffel bag. "What is it?" he asked, shifting his weight to one hip. "I'm on my way to the gym."

"We won't take much of your time," Faith said. "Let's talk in here." She led them into the salon and flicked on the light.

"Where were you today, Laura?" Griffith's gaze was curious.

Laura faked a tiny cough, holding her fist over her mouth. "I'm coming down with a cold, and I thought I'd nip it in the bud." That was the cover story they'd concocted regarding her absence.

Griffith drew back as though she'd announced she was carrying the bubonic plague. Perhaps Laura should have worn the bird mask. "Don't come near me. I want to stay healthy."

"Hence the gym, right?" Faith sat on a sofa and gestured for the others to sit.

Griffith sat in a chair and stowed his duffel between his feet. "I have to stay in shape. It's vital for my technique, which is very physical." Although seated, he puffed out his chest and tensed his arm muscles. Then he settled back and crossed an ankle over the opposite knee, his shoulders square.

Brother. Faith wanted to roll her eyes at the young man's egotism. "How are you holding up?" she asked in a soft voice. "I understand you and Audrey..."

Her compassionate question must have been unexpected, because naked emotion flashed in Griffith's eyes. He blinked back tears. "Um, not so good. I mean, Audrey and I were over a long time ago. And it wasn't that serious you know, but still."

Faith nodded. "It's always hard to lose a friend."

"Speaking of which," Laura said, "I wanted to ask you about Shaw."

A defiant light gleamed in Griffith's eyes. "He was no friend of mine. Sure, we grew up in the same small town, but we were never buddies."

Laura leaned forward in her seat, her posture intent. "I can understand that. Since Shaw gave your grandfather a heart attack."

As though echoing her words, Griffith slapped a hand onto his chest. His wide eyes revealed that Laura had scored a direct hit. "How did you know? Grandpa wanted to keep the whole thing quiet." His face twisted. "He's certainly a better man than I am."

"I didn't know," Laura admitted. "But I guessed. Someone said Shaw got in trouble for hurting an older man. And I remember your grandpa going to the hospital around that time."

Griffith rubbed the back of his neck, his gaze distant. "Yeah. We almost lost him. When I found out Shaw was responsible, I have to admit I wanted to kill him." His smile was lopsided. "But I didn't. That was over a decade ago."

Faith wondered if he was telling the truth. Had he finally

acted on a long-held grudge? But in that case, why kill Audrey? Or had Audrey's killer chosen to mimic the method of death to throw off investigators? She suppressed a groan. There were too many possible scenarios.

"Thanks for talking to us," Laura said. "I'm still determined to get to the bottom of his death. Shaw made a mistake back then, but he didn't deserve to die."

"Be careful. You never know what might happen when you poke a sleeping bear." Griffith's tone was ironic. He unfolded his limbs and stood. "Now if you'll excuse me, I'd like to go work out."

Once the young man had exited, whistling cheerfully as though he didn't have a care in the world, Faith stared at Laura. "What were you thinking? You may have just waved a red flag in front of a bull. What if Griffith is guilty? He has a motive—to avenge his grandfather."

Laura clapped a hand over her mouth. "You're right. I just get so angry about what happened to Shaw." Understanding dawned on her face. "It's strange that Griffith mentioned a bear. Maybe he was wearing the costume."

Even more reason for Laura to be careful. Faith believed the person in the costume had hit Laura and perhaps killed Audrey. She hoped they would solve the case soon before something else happened to Laura or another member of the troupe.

"There you are, Laura. I've been wondering how you are."

Faith and Laura turned to see Marlene entering the room.

Faith blinked. The normally chic assistant manager was dressed in a pink yoga outfit and sneakers, with her blonde hair in a ponytail. She looked younger and almost approachable.

"I'm doing pretty well," Laura said. "I rested all day."

Marlene sat on the chair Griffith had vacated. "Good. I'm glad to hear it. Don't rush coming back to work, okay?"

Who are you, and what have you done with Marlene? Faith wondered.

"Thank you." Laura gave Marlene grateful smile.

"It's too much liability for the manor to have injured employees on the job," Marlene said.

There's the Marlene we all know and love. Faith cleared her throat. "There is something I need to tell you." She quailed slightly under Marlene's chilly gaze and spoke quickly. "I've been asked to fill in for Audrey. It's only for the rest of the week, so it shouldn't impact my library duties too much. They're light right now anyway." Hearing herself babbling, she bit her tongue.

Marlene waved a hand. "That's fine. My concern is that the rest of the week goes off smoothly. Poor Mrs. Jaxon. This is one of her pet projects, and these foolish people go and get themselves killed."

Faith gulped back a sharp response. While she liked and respected Charlotte, the tragic deaths of Shaw and Audrey were far worse than a spoiled event, no matter how high-profile.

"Anyway," Marlene said, "that's not why I'm here." Once she had their expectant—or in Faith's case, apprehensive—attention, she said, "I've made a little progress on the matter you and I discussed, Faith."

She experienced relief, followed swiftly by annoyance. When would she stop letting the acerbic assistant manager get under her skin? "About Shaw's juvenile case?"

"Exactly. I'm hoping for more details, but I did learn something."

Faith took a deep breath as she waited for Marlene to continue.

"Shaw wasn't alone. But for some reason, the other children were never charged."

14

The pieces clicked together in Faith's mind, with the satisfaction of completing a puzzle. *Well, almost.* They still had to figure out who the other culprits were in case that had a bearing on Shaw's death.

"Is there a chance of getting more information?" Faith asked. "Of course, we're happy to get this much."

"My contact is going to try," Marlene said. "It's not easy as you know, since the records are sealed." She wrinkled her brow. "Shaw was only twelve when it happened."

Twelve! So young—barely out of childhood. Hearing that, Faith believed the pranks had surely started out as harmless. Not many twelve-year-olds were truly vicious.

Laura had been listening in silence. "The fact that other kids were there puts a whole new spin on everything."

Marlene got to her feet. "Heading in to dinner? We're doing a buffet in the breakfast room. Then I've got to get together with Brooke to plan the final banquet. Mrs. Jaxon wants it to be spectacular."

Lucky Brooke, meeting with Marlene after hours. But Faith merely smiled and said, "I'm sure the banquet will be fantastic with you and the kitchen staff in charge."

After a blessedly peaceful night, Faith awoke to the rattle of a food cart Brooke was pushing into the suite.

"Good morning," Brooke said, parking the cart beside Faith's bed. She lifted a silver cover to reveal eggs Benedict with shrimp and crabmeat.

"To what do I owe this lovely surprise?" Faith asked, pushing herself to a seated position. The savory aroma made her mouth water.

Brooke placed a bed tray across Faith's lap. "I thought you and Laura deserved a treat."

Next to Faith, Watson mewed plaintively.

Brooke smiled. "I didn't forget you, Watson. I've brought extra shrimp for you."

Faith laughed. "Shrimp? He'll never eat kibble again." She unrolled a napkin cylinder and extracted the silverware inside. "And I won't want to go home. You're spoiling me."

What would it be like to live at the manor? She sat back and allowed Brooke to place the main dish, a cup, and a glass of juice on the tray. A carafe of coffee followed by cream and sugar went on the bedside table. Watson's treats she placed on the fireplace hearth. He jumped off the bed to partake.

"Thank you," Faith said.

"My pleasure." Brooke wheeled the cart into the other bedroom.

Judging by the exclamations drifting through the open door, Laura was equally happy and grateful for Brooke's thoughtfulness.

Faith was deep into the meal when Brooke pushed the cart back out. "Put your empty dishes on this, and someone will come get it," she said. "I'd better get downstairs. We're doing a buffet at eight."

"A small but demanding group, right?" Faith commented. She spread peach jam on a slice of whole wheat toast.

Brooke exhaled, blowing her bangs up. "I'll say. And the banquet is going to be amazing. It'll include beef roasted over a fire pit and chowder cooked in cast-iron cauldrons. We're trying to create an authentic seventeenth-century feast."

"Rushes on the floor and lack of dining utensils too?" Faith quipped.

"No, not quite that authentic." Brooke grinned. "And thank goodness for our modern kitchen equipment, especially our commercial dishwasher. We're expecting over a hundred people."

Faith pictured the manor on that night, the last of the Everything Shakespeare event. They'd be performing *Romeo and Juliet* after the feast. "It's pretty exciting. Thanks again, Brooke. I'll see you downstairs later."

After devouring her delicious breakfast, Faith set her dishes on the cart and fished out her laptop. Settled back under the down coverlet with a fresh cup of coffee, she booted up a browser for a spot of research.

Laura wandered into the room, carrying a coffee mug. She sat on an armchair beside the fireplace.

Watson leaped onto Laura's lap.

"Traitor," Faith said to him.

"What are you up to?" Laura asked, motioning to Faith's laptop.

"I thought I'd do a little digging into people's backgrounds to see if I can find any clues regarding Shaw's and Audrey's deaths." Usually background research was one of her primary investigative tools. But she'd been so busy, she hadn't gotten around to it yet.

"Good idea." Laura gave a huge yawn, belatedly covering her mouth. "Sorry. I had the best night's sleep in ages." She ran a hand along Watson's back. "All due to this fella scaring off our prankster ghost."

Faith smiled at the new name for the spooky warbler. She turned back to the browser. Where to begin? First she typed in Shaw's name, but she found only brief mentions of his death. There was nothing about his past, and his social media page didn't tell her anything useful.

She had so many questions about the troupe, starting with the leader. *Bates Beaumont, what's your story?*

Laura set her coffee down and started a fire.

Faith tapped away to the comforting sound and warmth of crackling logs. Bates had been born to a wealthy family in the area, and he had attended the same schools as Charlotte's brother. He was a longtime fixture in the theatrical world but always in the second or third tier. His productions never quite made it to Broadway. In fact, most of his productions flopped, and Bates was usually one of the producers, which meant he'd most likely invested his own money.

Faith remembered an appropriate saying: "How do you make a small fortune in the theater? Start with a big fortune." She'd heard that ironic statement used to express the difficulty of various risky endeavors.

Aha. An in-depth magazine article about Bates and his *First Folio*. Faith scanned the story. It briefly mentioned his mysterious first wife, Beatrice, who had dropped out of sight in Europe. It had been a short marriage and, by all accounts, a disastrous one.

Beatrice had been an actress, and one of the photos was taken during a scene from a play. She and Bates were shown onstage confronting each other, the young woman wearing a Shakespeare costume.

Faith yelped.

Laura jumped. "Goodness! What was that for? Did you find something?"

"Come see this."

Laura obediently ambled over to the bed and peered at the screen Faith angled toward her.

"Doesn't she resemble Viola?" Faith asked.

Laura took a sip of coffee, studying the photo. "Kind of, I guess." She returned to her seat by the fire and picked up a magazine.

"Okay. I suppose that doesn't mean anything." Except that Bates cast young women who reminded him of his former wife.

Faith kept reading. The article went on to talk about the director's second wife, Imogen, who had died tragically in an accident a few years ago, leaving a daughter, Perdita, who had attended school on Cape Cod and a boarding school.

Something chimed in Faith's mind. "Did Perdita go to school in Turners Mills?"

Laura glanced up from her magazine. "Maybe. If she did, it was only for a little while." She smiled. "I'm pretty sure I would remember *her*."

"She is pretty striking." Faith bookmarked the article and began searching for information on the Turners Mills schools. From the article, she knew that Perdita was younger than Griffith, Corin, and Audrey. She found a classmates site that seemed promising, but she needed an account to access it. "Laura, can you help me?"

Laura set up an account and was able to view the various materials provided by other classmates at the high school. She giggled. "Look, there's a yearbook. I forgot about that." She opened the file, and together they browsed through the youthful faces.

They found Perdita's class first. And there was moody Perdita, a curtain of hair hiding most of her face.

Then they searched the older classes. Corin was cocky, a few dots of acne not dimming his bravado. Griffith was dark and intense. And Audrey was cute with corkscrew curls and a puzzled expression.

"I'll have to ask my sister if she remembers anything," Laura said. "She's pretty busy with her three kids and claims it's all a blur." She pointed out Bethany, a pretty blonde that Faith definitely would have guessed was related to Laura. "And that's Tucker, her husband."

Tucker was also blond, with regular features and an open smile.

"They must make an attractive couple," Faith observed.

"They do, and the kids are adorable. Do you believe they've been together since junior high?" Laura sighed. "It's disgusting how happy they are." Her eyes belied the statement, shining with pride and love.

"So where's Shaw?" Faith asked. She hadn't seen him among Bethany's classmates.

Laura navigated to another page, which had only group shots. "There he is."

Lanky Shaw stood in the back row, his distinctive mop of hair making him easy to pick out. He had slumped shoulders and a hangdog expression.

Faith's heart ached with sadness. "We've got to find out what happened. He doesn't look like the kind of kid who would hurt anyone."

"He wasn't," Laura said quietly.

A short while later, they put aside the laptop and got ready to go downstairs. Since this was Faith's first play as stage manager, she was both anxious and excited.

"I hope I don't blow it," she confided to Laura as they walked down the hallway.

Watson darted ahead, then stopped to wait for them.

Laura scoffed. "You won't. Did you see Audrey's binders? She has one for each play."

"I only saw the costume binder." The fact the former stage manager had been so organized was comforting. Perhaps Faith wouldn't make a hash of the production after all.

"I'll show you where they are." Laura laughed. "What's Rumpy up to now?" She had taken to calling Watson by his nickname, and he didn't seem terribly pleased to learn the unflattering name was spreading.

"It looks like he's spotted something," Faith said.

Watson paused by the junction of the main corridor to the side one where Laura had been found. He crouched low, whiskers twitching.

By mutual, unspoken agreement, the duo crept close along the wall as they approached the cat.

Faith's heart began a slow, heavy thudding, and dread seeped into her limbs. She hoped and prayed they wouldn't find yet another fatality.

They stopped beside Watson and peered down the hall.

Faith didn't spot any prone bodies, but she did see Perdita seated and facing the other way. She was conversing with an unfamiliar bald man who wore a heavy jacket, even though it was warm inside.

Most significantly, a bulky package lay on the accent table between them.

While Faith watched, Perdita put her hand on the package. She spoke in such a low voice that only snatches of what she said drifted to the listeners. "This is it . . . Let me know . . . I'll be in touch."

When Faith shifted slightly to get a better view, the floorboard creaked, a rarity at the manor.

In the back of her mind, Faith made a note to tell Marlene about it. As for the rest of her brain, it was paralyzed with the realization that Perdita had swung around to see the three of them lurking.

Perdita snatched up the package, her eyes blazing. "Do you mind? This is a private meeting."

"Sorry," Faith called. "We didn't mean to interrupt." There wasn't an explanation for their snooping, so she didn't offer one. Instead, they all retreated, practically running toward the staircase to the main floor.

A cold feeling began in Faith's stomach and spread to the rest of her. Had they just witnessed Perdita giving the Shakespeare *First Folio* to a buyer or a go-between?

15

"What do you think is going on?" Laura whispered as she and Faith descended the grand staircase.

Faith debated how much of her suspicions to tell Laura. But Laura worked in the library sometimes, and it was likely she would notice the rare book missing and raise the alarm.

"Perdita took the *Folio* out of the case," Faith said, keeping her voice low. "Her father knows and isn't concerned. But please keep it quiet."

Laura nodded. "You can count on me." Then she stopped short, her eyes wide. "Is Perdita selling it?"

It sure looks that way. "I have no idea. It's none of our business anyway," Faith said as much for her own benefit as Laura's. "Let's go or we'll be late."

They reached the bottom of the stairs and entered chaos.

Viola ran up and thrust a program at Faith. "You have to do something. They spelled my name wrong in tonight's program."

Faith scanned the paper. Viola's name was spelled *Piola*.

"They didn't notice *that*?" Laura snorted and snatched it from Faith's hand. "I'll take care of it." She marched away.

Then Griffith strode over, complaining about a costume mishap, and Corin was wondering if they could use real potted trees instead of the "ugly" fake ones for the boxtree scene. They had been damaged in transit.

Faith braced herself, sent up a prayer, and plunged in. Day one as stage manager had begun.

She finally had time to stop and breathe when the curtain rose and the performance of *Twelfth Night* began.

Griffith, as Orsino, reclined on the stage, pining for his love, Lady Olivia.

Wolfe, dressed as Sir Toby Belch, joined Faith on the edge of the stage, out of sight behind the curtains. "Good job. I knew you could pull it together."

"Barely," Faith said with a laugh. "Good thing Laura and Eileen were here to help me." Seeing that the performance was going smoothly, she asked, "Do you have a minute?" Gesturing for Wolfe to follow, they went into the empty dressing room.

"This thing is always slipping," he said, adjusting the false belly he wore under his costume. "So what's going on? I can tell something is wrong."

Faith stopped wringing her hands. "I saw Perdita meeting with a strange character earlier today. I think she may have given him the *Folio*."

"What exactly did you see?" Wolfe listened intently as Faith took him through the sequence of events. "Thanks for letting me know. I'll tell Bates, but of course it's up to him to deal with it. And his daughter."

"Of course." But Faith felt lighter now that Wolfe knew. The *Folio* wasn't her responsibility anymore. "There is another thing, but it's good news. Your ghost is gone. Watson frightened him away."

Wolfe crossed his arms and laughed. "I've got to hear this."

When she finished the tale, he said, "That's right. I was going to check on it for you. I thought we might still have speaking tubes left in place." A frown wrinkled his brow. "But that begs the question, who was trying to scare you?"

Whoever it was doesn't want us to learn the truth about Shaw. But now wasn't the time to go into that. Faith glanced at the wall clock. "We'd better get out there. You're on in a few."

The actors were taking curtain calls to thunderous applause when Laura received a text from her sister. She waved the phone at Faith. "I'm going to call her if that's okay. I asked her if she had any insights into our case."

"That's fine. But come back as soon as you can to help with the party." To go along with the theme of *Twelfth Night*, a light supper was being served in the banquet hall for the audience and the cast. This included a huge king cake made with fruit and nuts according an old English recipe.

Faith was swept along with the crowd toward the banquet hall. A troupe of jugglers hired for the evening was performing in the lobby, further snarling traffic. The staff once again wore jester hats, and wandering minstrels strummed lutes and played fiddles.

"Hello," someone said from behind her.

Startled, Faith whirled to see Wolfe grinning at her. He had ditched the belly but still wore medieval garb, as she did.

"Great turnout tonight." He had to raise his voice to be heard above a trio of drummers.

"It sure is." The festive atmosphere was exciting, and Faith felt her spirits lift. Or was her exhilaration due to the handsome man walking beside her?

When they entered the banquet hall, Faith noticed Charlotte and Bates standing near the colorful king cake, placed in a position of honor on its own table. Wolfe's mother was cutting the cake and putting the pieces onto small plates, and Bates handed them out.

"Are you hungry?" Wolfe asked. "The canapés look good."

A long table was set with platters featuring finger food, including mini mince and chicken pies, little rolls of beef with horseradish cream, and puff pastries with spinach and cheese.

Faith loaded a plate. She hadn't realized how hungry she was.

Eileen joined them. "The performance was wonderful." She smiled at Wolfe. "You had me in stitches, Sir Toby."

He bowed. "Thank you, milady. It was fun playing a role so far removed from my usual self."

A cry went up from near the cake table, and a wandering minstrel gave a blast on his trumpet.

"What's that all about?" Faith asked.

"Someone found the king in the cake," Eileen said. "A baby Jesus was hidden in the cake."

Crowns and fur-trimmed cloaks were produced, and a happy couple were crowned as king and queen of the night. By the laughter and joyous expressions, Faith could tell the festivities were a huge hit.

Where is Laura? She would love this frivolity. How long had she been gone?

Wolfe was summoned by his mother, and he slipped away with an apology.

"Have you seen Laura?" Faith asked Eileen.

"I haven't," Eileen said. "But in this crowd . . ." Her shrug said it all. The costumes, including wild medieval hats and veils, made it hard to pick out people.

Maybe she was catching up on family news. Faith knew what that was like. Sometimes she spoke to her mother so long, Faith found her ear numb and her phone red-hot when she hung up.

Eileen and Faith wandered around for a while, nibbling on refreshments, and then they watched the revelry from a table in the corner. The musicians banded together to play, and some of the guests began to dance.

"I can't imagine that the closing night will top this," Faith said. "It's fantastic."

"It sure is," Eileen said. "Castleton Manor continues to outdo itself with every event."

Faith glanced around for Laura, but she still hadn't shown up. Faith pulled out her phone, debating whether to send her a text. She really didn't feel like traipsing upstairs to see if she was in their suite.

Eileen laughed. "It's so incongruous to see you wearing that dress and holding a cell phone."

Faith smiled as she smoothed the skirt of the green-and-gold gown she was wearing. "I know. Even regular telephones weren't invented until three hundred years after women wore these styles."

Her phone buzzed in her hand.

It was a text from Laura. *Sorry, Faith. I'm out of here. I quit.*

Faith regarded the message with disbelief. Why would Laura quit her job right now? "No, it can't be." She pressed the icon to call Laura.

The phone rang and rang, then went to voice mail.

"Laura, it's Faith. What's happening? Let's talk before you make a decision, okay?" Faith valued Laura's assistance in the library, and she didn't want to lose her.

"What's going on?" Eileen asked.

Faith handed her the phone.

Eileen's mouth dropped open. "Isn't this rather sudden? I thought Laura seemed really happy working here. And with you."

"Me too." Faith's spirits sank. In a sudden decision, she pushed back her chair. "Let's go upstairs. Maybe she hasn't left yet."

Moving through the dense crowd was difficult, but they finally reached the hallway.

"Elevator or stairs?" Faith asked. She felt like running up the stairs, but she knew Eileen wouldn't be able to go as fast.

Her aunt waved a hand. "Go on ahead. I don't want to hold you back."

Taking Eileen at her word, Faith lifted her skirts and rushed down the hall. Then she took the grand staircase at a run, thankful her outfit was loose around the legs. The large skirt was one advantage of some medieval dresses.

The suite door was unlocked, which made Faith's heart leap in hope. Maybe Laura was still here.

But no, the rooms were empty, and all Laura's clothes and toiletries were gone. Only one lamp shone on the table where Diva and Bling swam in their bowl. Even Watson was out prowling around somewhere. The cat was probably lurking in the banquet hall, hoping for dropped tidbits.

Faith sank onto the bed. It didn't seem like Laura to make such a sudden decision and a hasty exit.

"Is she here?" Eileen stood in the doorway. She stepped inside and glanced around.

"No," Faith said sadly. "Something's wrong. Laura wouldn't do this."

Her aunt went to check out the fish, who circled excitedly when she appeared. "I know you don't want to think that. But take it from me, I've had a lot of employees at the library, and sometimes they do strange things. People can be impulsive. Or they have problems you don't know about."

"Maybe," Faith said, but she still wasn't convinced. Laura tended to be an open book, telling anyone who would listen what she thought and felt. She wouldn't have hidden a problem from Faith. It wasn't in her nature. She pulled out her phone and tried again, then threw it down onto the bed in disgust. "Right to voice mail."

Had Laura shut off the phone to avoid her?

Another text appeared. *Maybe it's Laura.* Faith snatched the phone up and read the message, her spirits plummeting. "It's Marlene. She wants to see me."

Eileen studied Faith, her normally twinkling eyes somber. "Do you think Marlene has something to do with Laura leaving?"

As they trudged back along the corridor, Eileen's remark grew fangs and latched on. *Marlene.* It had to be the assistant manager. She must have done something to upset the sensitive Laura.

Standing with arms folded, Marlene waited for them in the deserted Great Hall Gallery next to the statue of Agatha Christie. She wore a red velvet dress and a pointed hat trailing a veil.

A vision of Marlene as a classic witch flashed into Faith's mind. She clenched her fists, willing herself to calm down. Flying off the handle wouldn't help anyone, least of all Laura.

"Where have you been?" Marlene snapped as they approached. "You're supposed to be mingling with our guests."

Despite Faith's best resolutions, her criticism was like a match to tinder. "I was looking for Laura. What did you do to her? She needs this job to pay for college."

Marlene's hands went to her hips. "What are you on about now? I don't have time for this."

Faith found the text with fumbling fingers and held out the phone to Marlene. "She quit tonight. What happened?"

Marlene read the message with narrowed eyes. "I have no idea. But you know how young women are. *Flighty* isn't the word." She pushed the phone back at Faith. "I'm sorry. I know you liked her." Her stiff delivery implied that Faith was perhaps the only one.

Faith frowned in confusion. "So you didn't have an argument with Laura tonight?"

"No. I haven't seen her since after the play ended. And that was at a distance." Marlene gave a huff of exasperation. "Can we please drop the subject of an ex-employee? I have something to tell you."

Before she could continue, Perdita appeared from a nearby doorway, gliding across the floor with hands tucked inside the wide sleeves of her black robe. The wimple hiding her bright hair provided the clue that she was dressed as a medieval nun. To further the impression, she was whispering under her breath as if chanting prayers.

"Miss Beaumont?" Marlene asked.

Perdita jerked in surprise. "I didn't notice you standing there."

Marlene bit her lip, obviously struggling to hold back a retort. "How are you, Miss Beaumont? I hear there's dancing in the banquet hall."

"Is there?" Perdita reached up and adjusted her wimple. "I don't like dancing. I've been wandering around, enjoying the peace and quiet."

Peace and quiet? Tonight with all the music and chatter? "Have you seen Laura?" Faith asked.

Perdita gave her a blank stare.

"She's an employee of the manor," Faith explained. "Blonde, young, used to live in Turners Mills, like you."

"Oh, that Laura. Yes, I did see her. A while ago in the vestibule." Perdita smiled. "She was going outside with someone wearing that bird mask. So creepy."

"It is," Faith agreed. So Laura had been with one of the actors. What were they doing, going outside on a night like this? "Did you see which way they went?" Maybe the person had been helping Laura to her car.

"No. I didn't wait to find out." The young woman drifted away.

Once she was out of earshot, Faith asked, "What did you want to tell me, Marlene? I don't want to keep you any longer."

Marlene stared after Perdita. Instead of the usual scorn, distaste, or disgust, her features conveyed concern. "My contact called me tonight and told me Shaw wasn't alone when he tormented that old man. Audrey and Corin were there too."

Faith was too stunned to speak.

"In light of that," Marlene said, "I think Laura might be in trouble."

16

Faith reached out a hand and used the statue of Agatha Christie to prop herself up. The marble was cold under her skin. "You think someone might have *taken* Laura?" Or what if she was going to be murdered, like Audrey and Shaw?

"That's a bit extreme," Marlene said, frowning. "I just meant with her habit of diving into situations, she might be in hot water."

Even as Marlene tried to downplay the situation, Faith's head spun.

"Oh, there was something else," Marlene said. "Perdita was the one who turned in Shaw back then. She saw him running home after playing his prank."

Another piece of information twining the troupe together. Faith wondered how reliable Perdita was. Perhaps she was playing her own game. She remembered how Perdita had discovered both Shaw and Audrey. *Coincidence or something darker?*

Eileen put a hand on Faith's arm. "Let's go find Corin. If he's here, then most likely Laura left of her own volition and she's okay."

Faith saw the sense of that. "Thanks for telling us, Marlene," she managed to get out. "You might want to inform the police about what you learned in case it's related to the deaths."

As they started to walk away, Faith thought of something. "Can you please find Laura's emergency contact information? I want to see if her family knows where she is."

"I'm not your—" Marlene started. Then she relented. "I'll do that." An oddly vulnerable expression crossed her face. "And keep me posted, okay? I do hope Laura is all right."

"We will." Assuming they learned anything. A knot of dread hardened in Faith's belly. What if something terrible had happened to Laura?

The festivities were still going full force when Faith and Eileen returned to the banquet hall. Brooke and her team busily replenished the food the guests were gobbling up, and more people were dancing.

Wolfe spotted them and hurried over, beaming. He bowed in front of Faith. "Would you care to dance, milady?"

I sure would. But she couldn't, not with Laura missing. "Normally I would, but right now I need to talk to you. We're concerned about Laura." She gestured for him to step out into the much quieter hallway.

Faith told him about Laura's text and Perdita seeing her leaving the manor in the company of a masked person.

"It's regrettable if she did quit, but it happens." He raised an eyebrow. "I'm getting the impression there's more to it, though."

"There is," Faith said. "Laura vowed to find Shaw's killer. And we've just learned that Corin, Audrey, and Shaw were all involved in the juvenile case. Now two of them are dead." She shivered at hearing the situation so bluntly put.

"Is Corin a suspect or a possible victim?" Wolfe grasped the salient points quickly.

Faith threw up her hands. "We don't know. It was Griffith's grandfather they tormented into a heart attack."

"Let's locate Corin and Griffith," Wolfe said. "We'll also ask about Laura and see if anyone knows what happened or where she went."

A server went past, the bells on his jester hat bouncing.

Wolfe called for him to stop. "What kind of car does Laura drive?" he asked Faith. She gave him the information, and he relayed it to the young man. "Please check the employee parking lot, and let me know if that car is still there."

The server nodded and hurried off down the hallway.

Faith and her companions continued into the banquet hall and ran into Nell, who was on her way out.

"Good evening," the actress said. "Lovely party."

"I'm glad you're enjoying it," Wolfe said, his tone distracted. "Tell me. Have you seen Corin or Griffith lately, say within the half hour?"

Nell surveyed the bustling room. She waved an arm. "They're in there somewhere, I think. It wasn't my turn to keep track of them." She guffawed.

"How about Laura?" Faith asked. "The assistant stage manager. Did you see where she went?"

"That little mouse?" Nell wrinkled her nose. "You think she's off with Corin or Griffith?" She laughed again. "They're not interested in *her*, not as long as Lady Viola's in the room."

Faith held back the temptation to correct Nell's mistaken assumption. The fewer people who knew what was going on, the better.

Without another word, Nell grabbed her skirts and flounced past them.

"How rude," Eileen said with a frown, watching Nell walk away. "Laura's a lovely young woman."

"That's just Nell," Faith said. "It seems she has no control over her tongue."

"Let's split up and circle the room," Wolfe suggested. "We'll meet by the cake table. Don't say anything to Corin or Griffith about Laura being missing. Let's just find out if they're here or not."

Faith understood the wisdom of that, although they did need to talk to Corin at some point. But how could they do that without alerting him, if he was the killer?

Circling the room wasn't an easy task, since it involved weaving through groups of people and avoiding being bumped into or having one's toes stepped on. Behind a group of diners, Faith ducked under the arm of a burly man gesturing wildly and came face-to-face with Corin, heading her way.

Corin ran a hand through his hair, which was damp. A bandage was wrapped around his right index finger. "You startled me."

Faith attempted a laugh. "Same here." Her heart began to pound, and her chest tightened. "Nice event, isn't it?" Her voice was a squeak.

Corin gave her an odd look. "Sure is. If you'll excuse me . . ." He brushed past.

Faith was desperately tempted to ask him if he'd seen Laura, but she managed to refrain. Then she heard herself say, "How did your hair get wet?"

The actor ran his fingers through it again. "I went outside for some air, not that it's any of your business," he said. "It's snowing again."

Faith's cheeks heated. What a fool she was. "Oh. Sorry. What happened to your finger? Are you all right?"

Corin held it up and studied it as though surprised to see it injured. "This? I fell and cut it on the ice." He snorted. "Any other questions?"

She shook her head, feeling even more idiotic. "See you later." She wedged herself through a knot of people and kept moving. Now to find Griffith.

He was standing hand in hand with Viola near the roaring fireplace. Both of them had wet hair. Stepping outside for air seemed to be the order of the day.

Griffith reached out to Faith as she joined them. "Congratulate us. Viola and I are dating."

Viola elbowed him. "You're such an idiot. Why would Faith care about that?"

She didn't, but she had to admit it agreed with the normally intense actor. He was positively beaming, and his eyes were alight with joy. "I'm happy for you both. Have you been outside in the snow?" She touched her hair so they'd know what she was talking about.

"We were." Griffith tucked Viola's hand close to his side. "We went for a long walk in the garden."

"So romantic," Viola said, smiling at him. "I love the way the snow makes the topiaries look."

"Me too." Faith smiled wistfully. The manor's gardens were romantic every season of the year and under all conditions.

Glancing around, Faith saw Wolfe and Eileen waiting for her near the few crumbs that remained of the king cake. She took a deep breath and asked, "You didn't run into Laura outside by any chance? I can't find her, so I wonder if she left." She tensed as she waited for the answer, hoping she wasn't making a mistake asking about Laura.

The couple stared at each other, shaking their heads.

"We didn't see anyone," Griffith said. He laughed. "No one else is crazy enough to venture out in the cold when it's so nice and warm in here."

Faith nodded and moved on.

"I found Corin and Griffith," Faith announced when she joined Wolfe and Eileen. "Strangely, they'd both been outside." She passed along the gist of the conversations.

"I'm not sure where to go from here," Wolfe said. "We have no proof a crime was committed."

"No, just a bad feeling." Faith felt her phone buzz in her pocket and pulled it out. A text from Marlene flashed on the screen. "Good. Marlene gave me Laura's family's contact information." Phone numbers for Laura's mother and sister were listed. "Excuse me while I call her sister. Laura was talking to her tonight."

Faith stepped out into the hall and dialed the number, praying she'd get a response. Then she froze. What could she say that wouldn't alarm Bethany?

An idea popped into her mind just as a young woman answered after three rings. In the background, a child wailed. "Hello?"

Faith raised her voice in order to be heard. "Is this Bethany? I'm Faith Newberry from Castleton Manor. Laura used to work here."

The wailing grew fainter, suggesting Bethany had walked to a quieter room. "Oh yeah. I remember her mentioning you." Her voice was placid, which hinted that Laura hadn't vented to her, about Faith at any rate. Then there was a pause. "You said *used* to work there?"

Her sister doesn't know. What does that mean? "Yes. You see, I got a text from Laura a little while ago saying she quit." Faith chose her words carefully. "I've been trying to get in touch with her, but her phone must be dead. I have some things of hers that she needs to pick up at her convenience."

Silence, except for the faint crying. "I'm really surprised to hear this. When I spoke to Laura earlier, she was all bubbles about her job." Another pause. "But of course I'll pass along the message when I talk to her."

"Please do. Have her call me right away, okay? I want to check in and be sure she's doing well."

Wolfe and Eileen had wandered out to the hall and were standing nearby.

Faith disconnected the call with a groan. "Her sister doesn't know where she is."

The staff member Wolfe had sent to the parking lot came trotting down the hall, his bells jingling. "The car is gone, Mr. Jaxon," he said. Then he disappeared into the banquet hall, headed back to his duties.

Wolfe's gaze was distant. "It looks like Laura left. I'm not sure there's anything else we can do right now. There isn't any evidence she's come to harm."

The feeling of dread in Faith's belly intensified. "I can't stand this. Evidence or not, my gut is telling me something is wrong." She heard the fretful, frightened tone in her voice and bit her lip. This was her boss she was talking to.

Eileen put a gentle hand on her arm. "Let's go back up to the room. Maybe we'll discover a clue or something."

"Do that," Wolfe said. "And let me know if you find anything." His blue eyes bored into Faith's. "If she doesn't turn up by morning, either here or somewhere else, I promise I'll launch a search."

Tension rushed out of Faith's body at his words. "Okay, thanks. We'll keep you posted."

"Let's take the elevator," Eileen said. "I can't face the stairs."

Faith and Eileen hurried to the elevator.

The doors were closing when Watson darted inside.

"Rumpy!" Faith said with a laugh. "That's a dangerous trick."

"I'm sure he had it timed just right," Eileen said.

Faith bent to stroke his back. "You're wet. Were you outside getting air like everyone else?"

In answer, he rubbed against her dress as though trying to dry off.

A few minutes later, they entered the suite again. Brooke was still downstairs, tied up with the late evening supper. Faith and Eileen went into the second bedroom to see if they could find anything this time.

Both beds had been made up, and the spreads hung to the floor. Watson disappeared under Laura's bed while Eileen checked the wardrobe.

Faith opened the bedside table. There was nothing inside. She shut the drawer with a sigh.

Watson was wrestling with something on the floor, making the bedspread bell out and hit her feet.

"Cut it out," Faith said, reaching down to lift the fabric. She really didn't want him to leave holes with his claws.

The cat lay on his side, paws protectively clutching a long yellow sock.

"Laura must have left that," Eileen said.

Faith gently tugged the sock away from Watson's grip, an idea flashing into her mind. "This reminds me of something." Then it came to her. "Corin wore stockings of this color in the play tonight."

Is this a clue? A deep certainty filled Faith's heart. Laura might be scatterbrained sometimes and a little clumsy, but when it came to her personal belongings, Faith had noticed she was neat and tidy.

"Corin had something to do with her leaving," Faith said, waving the sock.

Watson scrambled to his feet and dashed to the suite door. His meow was long and loud.

Faith recognized that sound. It meant, "Follow me."

17

"Come on. Let's go." Faith grabbed her winter coat and slipped on a pair of boots.

"You think Watson is leading us outside?" Eileen asked. "Maybe Laura is somewhere in the building."

Watson yowled again, a screeching sound that set Faith's nerves on edge.

"Possibly," Faith replied. "But if not, I don't want to take the time to come back up."

"Good point." Eileen slipped on her fleece-lined boots and puffy jacket, which she'd worn to the manor earlier and left in Faith's suite. "I'm ready."

Faith opened the suite door. "Go on, Watson. Do your thing."

The cat padded down the hall, pausing occasionally to let them catch up. With unerring resolve, he led them through the lobby and the Great Hall Gallery to the French doors lining the loggia. He sat and waited for Faith to open one of the doors to let them out into the gardens beyond.

Cold wind and blowing snow greeted them when they stepped out onto the loggia.

Faith winced, ducking her head. "I hope you're sure about this, Rumpy."

Watson twitched his stub of a tail. He glanced at them over his shoulder, green eyes gleaming, and trotted down the steps, which had been cleared of fresh snow.

Faith was grateful the manor was so well maintained as she descended the steps without fear of slipping and falling.

At the bottom of the stairs, Watson headed down a path in the opposite direction from the gardener's cottage. It led to an area of the grounds Faith had rarely explored. They skirted the manor, crossed a delivery driveway, and went into the woods.

Faith glanced back at the manor with a shiver. The lights in the mansion were quickly receding.

"Where is he taking us?" Eileen asked. She was being a trouper, keeping up with the cat without complaint.

"I have no idea," Faith said. She kept her attention on the snow, the trail a visible path of white between thick rows of trunks pressing close on each side.

"Well, at least we're not heading toward the cliffs," Eileen said, evidently trying to inject a little levity. "So we should be okay."

The woods ended at another driveway. By the looks of it, a car had passed by recently. The treads were still discernible despite the drifting snow.

Without pausing, Watson turned left and began trotting down the road.

"Where does this go?" Eileen asked, struggling over the snowbank.

Faith reached out a hand to help her. "I don't know." In her mind, she tried to picture where they were on the property. This lane was most likely an offshoot of the service drive.

Watson's tiny figure was a speck of black against the snow. Once in a while a streetlamp shone overhead. After about ten minutes of trudging, an enormous building loomed out of the dark. The sodium light hanging on the front revealed it was a barnlike garage.

Understanding dawned. "I'll bet this is where the Jaxons keep their cars," Faith said. Various members of the family, including Wolfe, enjoyed collecting vintage or interesting vehicles. She'd heard people reference the collection that was kept here at the manor.

"Is Laura inside that building?" Eileen's face creased in puzzlement.

"Watson seems to think so."

He stood in front of a door, face tipped up, as though waiting for someone to let him in.

Faith tested the door handle and wasn't surprised to discover it was locked.

"Now what?" Eileen asked, shifting from foot to foot. "It's cold out here."

Watson hadn't budged from his spot.

"I'm calling Wolfe." Faith dug out her phone and dialed.

Wolfe answered immediately. "Did you find something?" he asked anxiously.

"We're out by your huge garage," she said. "And I think Laura might be inside. But it's locked so I can't check."

"I'll be right there."

After a few minutes of stomping their feet and swinging their arms to stay warm, Faith heard the engine of a vehicle.

Lights bounced along the road, and Wolfe's BMW came into view. He pulled up beside them and rolled down the driver's side window. "What led you two here?"

Faith pointed at Watson, who was gazing up at Wolfe. She explained what had happened, her words tumbling out in a rush. "I've learned the hard way to trust my cat," she concluded. "He's helped me more than once."

Wolfe nodded. "I know. Though what Laura would be doing here, I can't imagine." He pointed a controller at the building, and one of the doors opened. Then he drove inside, proceeded straight ahead into a vacant spot, and switched off the engine.

As the trio entered, Wolfe emerged from the car, dressed for the weather in a thick down jacket and a wool hat. He flicked a switch on the wall, then pressed the controller to shut the door.

The vast garage was filled with at least a dozen cloth-covered vehicles. Workbenches lined two sides of the room, with tools neatly hung on the walls or stored in tall rolling chests. A blower went on overhead, sending welcome warm air throughout the building.

Watson stalked off and began sniffing around the perimeter of the building, his usual behavior in a new place.

There was no sign of Laura.

"What now?" Eileen asked.

"Let's search," Wolfe said. He lifted the cover of the nearest car, a gorgeous silver Corvette. "Maybe she's inside one of the vehicles."

Faith's belly clenched. *In what condition?* Pushing down her fear, she reached for the closest cover, lifting it enough to peek inside the windows. Empty.

Eileen squawked. When the other two looked at her, she said, "I don't think this car belongs here." She ripped the rest of the cover off, revealing a tiny sedan.

Faith ran over and checked the plate number. "This is Laura's car." Peering closely, she saw a few wet spots on the cement floor. The car had been parked in the garage very recently. She peered inside. A pair of mittens and a hat she recognized as Laura's lay on the console.

Wolfe joined them. "I don't understand. Why would Laura's car be in here?"

"Because someone wants us to think she left the manor," Faith answered. She glanced around the big building. There wasn't an upstairs she could see. "So where is she?" She fervently hoped the young woman hadn't been moved to another location.

Light shone in Wolfe's eyes. "I have an idea. Come with me."

Wolfe led the way to the back of the building and into the shadowy recesses near the workbenches. He flipped on another light, then hunkered down and lifted a ring set in a trapdoor. "There used to be storage down here before another outbuilding was built."

The recess under the building was pitch-black, with only a few steps of a staircase visible.

Wolfe hunted around on a bench and found a flashlight. "Let me go down first," he said. Swinging the light, he descended into the darkness.

Watson came out from under the nearest vehicle and followed him down.

Faith reached out and grabbed Eileen's hand. *What will he find?* Faith sent up prayers for Laura, for her safety and well-being.

"Come on down," Wolfe called. "She's here. And she's okay."

The rush of relief was so sweet, Faith practically tasted it. She gestured toward the opening. "Go ahead. After you."

Eileen shook her head. "It's too steep for me."

Faith stepped toward the opening, reaching out to grip the edge. After a dozen steps, she reached the bottom.

Wolfe and Watson were sitting beside Laura, who lay on a heap of blankets, duct tape around her wrists and ankles and across her mouth. Wolfe was trying to ease away the duct tape on her face.

When Laura saw Faith, she kicked and grunted, her eyes wide with excitement.

Faith ran to her side and knelt, heedless of the hard-packed dirt floor. "I'm so glad you're okay." Tears sprang to her eyes, and she wiped them away with the back of her hand.

Tears welled up in Laura's eyes too, and she grunted again.

"Faith, can you get me a bottle of adhesive remover from the bench upstairs?" Wolfe asked. "It will make taking off the tape much less painful."

"Just a minute." Faith returned to the main floor and quickly found the bottle. She filled Eileen in and went back down.

"Close your eyes," Wolfe instructed. He gently squirted the compound on the tape across Laura's skin. Then he removed the gag with ease.

Laura stretched her mouth wide. "Oh, that feels so much better."

Wolfe pulled out a pocketknife and began sawing at the tape around her wrists.

"What happened?" Faith asked, taking a seat on the floor next to Laura. "We were worried." She hugged what she could reach of the young woman.

"It was Corin," Laura said. "He told me he knew who killed Shaw and wanted to show me proof." Her face crumpled into a frown. "He said it was Griffith and he'd been secretly using this garage to prepare the poison. Once he got me here, he tied me up."

"How did Corin know about this building?" Wolfe asked. He finished with her wrists and moved on to her ankles.

"Corin was here when he was a kid," Laura explained. "With Perdita."

"I remember that visit," Wolfe said. "But not the kids, I'm afraid."

Eileen ventured down a couple of steps. "Someone's coming. I saw the lights of a vehicle on the road." She pressed her lips together in satisfaction. "I put the cover back on Laura's car and turned off the front overhead lights just in case."

"Good thinking," Wolfe said. "Can you make it down here? I want you safe." He ran for the stairs and helped the older woman navigate the steps down to the cellar.

Laura put a hand to her mouth. "What are we going to do?"

Wolfe ran up the stairs. "Leave it to me."

Watson followed Wolfe.

"Rumpy, stay down here," Faith said.

Naturally, the cat didn't obey.

Faith shook her head and rose. "I'm going up to keep an eye on things."

"Be careful," Eileen warned.

"Call 911," Faith said. She tossed her phone to Eileen. Moving swiftly, she crept up the stairs. She found a vantage point near Laura's car where she could watch the confrontation.

The door opened, and a figure stepped inside, reaching for the light switch.

"Hold it." Wolfe's voice boomed out in the darkness. He switched on a flashlight, shining it right into Corin's eyes. "What are you doing here?"

Squinting, Corin raised his hands. "Whoa. Don't do that, man. I was just coming to check out the cool rides."

If Faith hadn't known the truth, she might have been convinced by his persona of wounded, harmless goodwill.

"How did you get in here?" Wolfe asked. "Keys are restricted."

The actor shuffled his feet. "Ah, well, one of the staff—" With a growl, he launched himself at Wolfe.

The two men tumbled to the floor, fists flying.

Faith froze, not sure what to do. Wolfe was strong, but Corin was younger and apparently imbued with the strength of the insane. Watching them tussle, her heart raced, and her breath came in gasps.

She glanced around, her gaze skittering. How could she help? Thoughts flitted through her mind and vanished. The familiar symptoms of panic.

Panic. Now there's an idea.

She wrenched open Laura's car door and dived inside. Fingers shaking, she grabbed the key fob and pressed the panic button. An earsplitting *whoop-whoop-whoop* resounded in the echoing space. The car lights flashed.

The sudden distraction gave Wolfe the edge he needed. With a massive effort, he flipped Corin over and pinned him down by sitting on him and holding his wrists.

Once she saw Wolfe was in control, Faith pressed the fob again, and blessed silence reigned. "What can I do?" she called.

"Get me some rope," Wolfe said, panting. He nodded to indicate where it was. "On the back wall."

Corin struggled to get up.

"Don't move a muscle," Wolfe warned.

As Faith hurried to the back, car tires crunched on the snow, and flashing red and blue lights lit up the interior of the barn. The police had arrived.

"Never mind about the rope," Wolfe called. "We've got something better coming."

"You can't have me arrested," Corin snarled. "I didn't do anything."

Wolfe's laugh was disbelieving. "We'll have the police sort that out, shall we?"

By the time Faith joined the duo, Chief Garris and Officer Laddy were entering the garage.

Laddy flicked on the overhead switch, his mouth dropping open briefly when he saw the covered automobiles. Then he stood at attention behind his boss.

"Wolfe, what's going on?" Garris asked. He eyed Corin, who was standing now, with Wolfe gripping one of his shoulders.

Corin tried to twist away. "Nothing. I came out here to see the cars, and he attacked me."

"Wolfe?" Garris asked, obviously regarding him as a more accurate source of information.

"This young man kidnapped one of our staff members. We also think he's involved in the murders of Shaw Hastings and Audrey Crowe."

The actor scoffed. "How can you call it kidnapping if someone drives you somewhere? She brought me here in her car."

Despite Corin's bravado, Faith noticed a trickle of sweat on his forehead.

"How about tying me up with duct tape and leaving me in the cellar?" Laura's voice came from the rear of the building. "My legs are still numb."

Laura and Eileen came into view, supporting each other.

"Unlawful restraint at least," Laddy said. "Shall we take him in?"

The chief nodded.

Laddy read Corin his rights while cuffing him.

"Add trespassing and assault," Wolfe said. "Faith witnessed the whole thing."

Faith nodded. "It's true. Corin came here and attacked Wolfe when he asked what Corin was doing." Then she said, "Corin was there when Shaw tormented an older man years ago in Turners Mills. So was Audrey. Now two of them are dead."

Corin's laugh sent a shiver up her spine, like something out of a horror movie. "Don't forget there's one other person involved. Griffith. The old man was his grandfather after all." His smile was sly. "Maybe you should talk to him. I'd do it pretty quickly."

18

A pause met Corin's words.

Then Officer Laddy said, "Quit messing around. You're coming with me." The officer took one of Corin's restrained arms and maneuvered the young man out the door.

"Laddy will book him at the station while I take statements," Garris said.

"Let's go up to the house," Wolfe suggested. "It's much more comfortable." He glanced at Laura. "I'm sure you'd appreciate getting out of here."

She rubbed her wrists, which still showed red marks from the tape. "I sure would. I was really scared. Thanks for rescuing me." As she gave each of them a brief hug, her eyes brimmed over with tears.

Faith knew that feeling, the relief of tension after an ordeal. She gave Laura another hug, then asked, "Did Corin actually confess to killing Shaw and Audrey?" The actor's gibe had lodged in her mind. Was he saying that Griffith was guilty? Or that he was in danger?

"No," Laura said, accepting a tissue from the ever-prepared Eileen. "He lured me downstairs, saying he had information about the murders, then tied me up. Said he needed me out of the way for a while."

Garris listened intently. "Let's save this for an official statement, okay? I'll meet you up at the house." He strode with purpose to the door and exited the garage.

Wolfe pressed the garage door button, and the door behind his BMW rose smoothly. "Climb in, everyone. Let's go."

Watson appeared and rubbed against his legs.

"You too, Rumpy." Wolfe grinned at Faith, and she was grateful for this touch of humor. She hadn't known he'd picked up on her pet's nickname.

As for Watson, he merely regarded Wolfe with a stare before leaping gracefully into the front seat.

"Is it just me, or did that look clearly say, 'Et tu, Brute?'" Wolfe asked.

"That's how I interpreted it," Faith said with a laugh.

Back at the manor, Wolfe suggested they gather in the library. Chief Garris could conduct private interviews in the den nearby. "Can you please have the kitchen bring us hot drinks and a snack?" Wolfe asked Faith once they were inside.

"Sure, I'll go find Brooke." Faith didn't mind the errand. It gave her a chance to gather her thoughts and also update her friend on what had happened.

In the banquet hall, staff members were cleaning up the remains of the party.

Brooke spotted Faith and rushed across the wood floor, her shoes squeaking. "Where have you been?" she asked, wiping her hands on her apron. "You've been gone for ages."

"It's a long story," Faith said. She quickly gave her friend the highlights.

Brooke made gratifying exclamations and interjections as she listened.

"Chief Garris is getting ready to interview everyone, so I was sent for refreshments." Faith glanced around the empty room. All the remaining food had been put away. "Do you mind? You must be exhausted."

"It's fine," Brooke said. "I want to be doing something anyway. Let's go down to the kitchen."

As they walked across the room, Corin's words floated into Faith's mind again. *Don't forget there's one other person involved. Griffith. The older man was his grandfather after all.* "Do you know where Griffith is?"

Brooke put a hand on her chest. "Oh, it's so romantic. He and Viola are having a midnight supper in his room. We just sent up a meal, including a special lover's punch."

Faith broke into a run. "Let's go," she called over her shoulder. "I think they may be in danger."

To her relief, Brooke didn't question her.

The pair pounded along the hallway to the staircase and up, taking the steps two at a time.

"Which suite is he in?" Brooke asked when they reached the second floor.

"I have no idea." Faith paused as she heard faint sounds of classical music leaking into the hall. "But I know someone who does." She crossed the hall and knocked on Marlene's door.

The assistant manager answered, thankfully not wearing skin products on her face this time. Or at least from what Faith could see through the tiny crack in the door. "Yes?" Soaring strains of Mozart filled the air.

"Which suite is Griffith in?" Faith clenched her fists as she waited for the answer. They didn't have time to go down to the lobby and check in the system.

"The Charles Dickens Suite. Why?" The door opened wider, revealing Marlene, elegant in marabou-trimmed lounging pajamas.

"He may be in trouble." Faith didn't linger. She took off again.

Brooke was already running down the corridor toward the suite.

It took a few knocks to get an answer at the Dickens suite. If it hadn't been a possible matter of life and death, Faith would have felt like a real heel, interrupting the couple's private time.

"Can I help you?" Griffith sounded like he hoped not.

Behind him, near the fireplace, Viola sat at a charming table for two. She raised a glass of ruby-red liquid to her lips.

"No!" Faith barged into the room, pushing an obviously surprised Griffith aside. "Don't drink that!"

Viola started, splashing the liquid onto the snow-white tablecloth, where it made red blotches. She set the glass down with shaking hands.

"You didn't drink any of the punch, did you?" Faith asked, fully aware that the couple were staring at her as if she had lost her marbles. "We think it might be poisoned."

"The biggest clue was that Corin wanted Laura out of the way," Faith said to Chief Garris later. "Why? He was going to kill someone else."

She was sitting at the table in the den with the chief, Laddy, Wolfe, Griffith, Eileen, Brooke, and Laura.

The forensics team had arrived and had taken custody of the punch. After a search of Corin's room revealed a supply of yew branches and equipment to liquefy them into poison, his charges had been upgraded to two counts of first-degree murder and two counts of attempted murder.

They'd also found notes that appeared to be from Shaw, demanding money to keep quiet about Corin's involvement in Griffith's grandfather's heart attack.

"So Corin dropped the stage light, hoping to hit Shaw," Faith said. "And when that didn't work, he slipped the poison into Shaw's root beer when no one was paying attention."

Garris nodded.

"Why did Corin do it?" Eileen asked. "It's been over a decade since the incident."

"I can answer that," Griffith said. "He told me he was on the short list for a major Broadway play. I'm guessing he couldn't afford any bad press. They would dump him in a minute."

"It's sad," Laura said. "Shaw was just a kid back then and too scared to rat the other two out. Now I guess he saw a chance to make Corin pay after all these years. And Shaw really needed the money. He was trying to save up for college, but he was in a lot of debt."

Faith nodded. That explained why Shaw had gotten a loan from the manor and was asking others for money.

"And Audrey fell afoul of Corin somehow?" Wolfe guessed.

Griffith's expression was sorrowful. "I didn't know for the longest time that Audrey had been involved. After I found out—from Shaw—well, it really put an end to our relationship, such as it was. She told me that scaring Gramps was the biggest mistake of her life, and she'd spent the past decade trying to atone for it. When she died, I thought she'd killed herself out of remorse." He paused. "Now it appears she was too big a risk for Corin."

The room was silent for a long moment.

Faith's heart was grieved for the victims—and thankful Laura, Griffith, and Viola hadn't joined them.

"On a lighter note," Wolfe said, "we're going to be down an actor for the last two plays. If we're done here, I'd better go see what Bates wants to do. Rehearsals for *The Winter's Tale* are tomorrow. And then we've got the finale, *Romeo and Juliet*, two days after that."

Laddy examined his fingernails in a studied yet casual way. "I might be able to help you with that, Mr. Jaxon. I've got a little acting experience."

Faith remembered that Laddy had acted in a film shot at the manor, but Corin's parts were much more involved and difficult than the role Laddy had played.

"I think that's an excellent idea," Eileen said. She'd been silent until now, and by the startled glances she received, most of the others had forgotten she was even there. She turned to Wolfe. "I remember Bryan performing in Shakespeare plays when he was in school. He'll do just fine."

"Isn't Officer Laddy amazing?" Brooke stopped to talk to Faith while the cast was rehearsing the next afternoon. She sighed, clasping her hands like a lovestruck maiden. "He's so gorgeous too."

Bates had decided on a dress rehearsal, and the officer was cavorting in tights and a doublet, giving a spectacular performance as several of the characters from Shakespeare's acclaimed play.

"You're right on both matters," Faith said.

Away from his official duties, Officer Laddy was funny, quick-witted, and quite adept at acting. Nell especially seemed impressed by his charm and good looks.

Brooke leaned on the cart she was pushing. "Whew. I am so tired. Two more performances and this event will be over."

"Same here," Faith said with a sigh. Of course, having two murders, a kidnapping—no matter what Corin claimed—and the mysterious removal of a rare book hadn't made things easier. At this point, Faith felt like she was battling stormy seas, fighting to get to shore.

Which, in this case, represented a few days off and an upcoming excursion to Boston. Eileen, Brooke, and Midge would be going. "I can't wait for our trip," Faith said. "Did I tell you Laura is coming with us?"

Brooke grinned. "I'm so glad. She deserves a nice getaway as much as the rest of us, if not more."

Later that evening, Faith trudged upstairs, Watson at her heels, looking forward to a hot bath and a good book. Laura was in the billiard room with the rest of the cast. But Faith needed some time alone, even if Brooke and Laura were dear friends.

She stopped short in the upper hallway, thinking of something that sounded even better. "Watson, let's go home."

After packing up a few things and sending a text to Brooke and Laura, she made her way out of the quiet manor. The stage was ready for the performance of *The Winter's Tale*, and Faith paused to regard the waiting set with satisfaction. She could imagine the seats filled with people enjoying the dramatic play, so perfect for this time of year.

As she opened the French door, Watson froze. He glanced back over his shoulder at something in the shadows.

"Come on," Faith urged. "We're letting all the heat out."

The cat started moving again, and they stepped out under starstrewn skies. The rising moon made a golden path on the bay, the waters glassy on this still night.

Fortunately, the path to the cottage had been cleared so Faith didn't have to wade through deep snow. They wound their way past empty fountains and looming, snow-covered topiaries.

They were beside the topiary of two little girls reading when Watson stopped again. This time he crouched with a hiss, facing into the heart of the garden.

Unease trickled down Faith's spine. Was someone—or something—out there? Perhaps a nocturnal animal was roaming. A deer or a fox, even. They didn't hibernate.

Something flickered in the topiaries. A flash of white.

Acting on instinct, she hoisted her bag more firmly onto her shoulder and began to trot. Wearing heavy boots, that was as fast as she dared to go. Even so, she was in danger of tripping and sprawling headlong into cold, wet snow.

The shortcut. Faith spotted the familiar opening between two spruce trees. She charged into the narrow gap, only to find herself creating a small avalanche of snow from the branches. Buckets of snow cascaded down, falling down her neck and filling her boots.

She was trapped in snow above her knees. The white flickering she'd seen moved closer, darting between the trees.

Watson growled and hissed.

The moonlight illuminated the creature, revealing the bird mask.

A jolt of fear galvanized Faith, and she thrashed her feet up and down, trying to release them from the clinging, soft drift. "Who are you? Go away."

In response, the bird mask moved even closer, the huge pointed beak particularly sinister in the moonlight.

Watson gave an unearthly scream, reminding Faith of a panther. Moving lightly on top of the snow, he charged toward the stalker, his silent, steady movements even more bone-chilling than his cry.

"Stop him!" The bird mask flew off, revealing a cowering Nell. "Don't let him scratch me."

"Rumpy." Faith's tone was stern.

Although the cat often ignored her directives, this time he thankfully listened. He halted, dropped to his haunches, and began to groom as if to say, "Who? Me? I wasn't doing anything."

Faith finally wrested her feet free. Ignoring the cold burn of melting snow on her feet, she stomped toward Nell. "What's the big idea, scaring me that way? It's not funny."

Nell's shamed expression was plain in the strengthening moonlight. "I'm sorry. I was only having a bit of fun. It's so boring around here that I'm ready to go round the bend."

Boring was not the word Faith would assign to the manor. "Are you the one who used the speaking tubes to scare us?" She'd guessed that from Watson's reaction. "And messed around with the bear suit?"

"Yes and yes." Nell wrung her hands, which were clad in thick mittens.

"How did you get into our room?" Faith persisted.

"I borrowed a key from the front desk," Nell admitted.

"Did you also rip Viola's dress and tape the scroll to the Agatha Christie statue?"

Nell nodded. "But it wasn't me the day that light fell to the floor. I swear it."

"I didn't think so," Faith said. "I've got to get going. Long day tomorrow."

From this vantage point, Faith saw the lone light burning at the cottage. She headed in that direction with relief, more eager than ever for that hot bath.

Behind her, Nell called, "You might think I'm strange. But you'd better be careful. More trouble is afoot."

19

The rest of the way to the cottage, Nell's warning rankled in the back of Faith's mind. *How annoying.* She couldn't even enjoy a night to herself without someone spoiling it.

Faith added a generous dollop of bubble bath to the tub, grabbed the most mindless magazine she could find, and lit a lavender-scented candle. No more worries. This was her time. And Watson's.

He jumped onto the commode and curled up on the seat. His purr was loud and comforting.

"Good job," she said, her heart swelling with warmth for the tuxedo cat. He was a wonderful partner in solving crimes. And in taking care of mischief-makers too.

What did Nell mean by "More trouble is afoot"? She shook her head, ending that train of thought.

Faith opened the magazine and read about spring fashions. Ah, gauzy floral dresses and sandals. They were something to look forward to in the dead of winter.

Pandemonium greeted Faith and Watson when they reached the Great Hall Gallery the next morning.

Workers were up on ladders, some tearing down decorations while others put up new ones. The rows of chairs had been moved aside, and a team of cleaners was polishing the already glossy floor.

Watson scampered off, no doubt to seek his own adventures.

Charlotte and Marlene came sweeping up to Faith, clipboards in hand.

"Good morning," Charlotte said, smiling. "We've had some exciting news. Sid Meyers is returning tonight to film *The Winter's Tale*. So we're redecorating, making everything fresh."

"He said he has a major surprise to announce tonight," Marlene added. Her dry tone revealed what she thought of that, despite her smile. Marlene hated surprises.

"How wonderful," Faith said faintly. Inside she was quaking, hoping and praying she wouldn't make any mistakes recorded for posterity. With her lack of experience, she was definitely the weak link.

"After so much tragedy, I do want the week to end on a good note," Charlotte continued, her brow creased with concern. "If tonight goes well, they'll return to film *Romeo and Juliet* and our gala evening. And then perhaps they'll do the series Sid has been discussing with Bates."

"I hope so," Faith said, meaning it. The poor producer had suffered enough. She pushed up the sleeves of her sweater. "Put me to work. I want to help."

Hours later, the hall looked like an enchanted winter wonderland. The balconies and columns were decorated with white garlands twined with colored lights. Woodland creatures made from strands of white lights stood in groups near pure white evergreen trees. There were even swans on a mirror pond surrounded by fluffy fake snow.

"We're going to have trouble competing onstage," Wolfe said to Charlotte. He had joined the small group admiring their work. "No one will be watching us."

His mother laughed. "I don't think so. The performances have been captivating. And it doesn't hurt that the plays are abridged. With today's short attention spans . . ."

The rumbling of wheels was heard, and a group of technicians entered the hall, Sid Meyers and Bates leading the way. The television crew had arrived.

"Ready or not," Wolfe said, grinning at Faith, "the show must go on."

Eileen had returned to help with costumes, and between her and

Laura, the cast was outfitted appropriately and on time. But that didn't mean there wasn't a last-minute fit of nerves in the dressing room.

"I look awful!" Viola wailed, pointing to an almost invisible dot on her skin. "Someone help me."

"I'll do it," Eileen said. "I'm pretty good with concealer." She cracked a smile. "At my age, you have to be."

"Cut it out," Faith chided her. "You're gorgeous."

Faith was in the middle of pinning up Perdita's hair. With the departure of Corin, Perdita had been drafted into service to ease the burden on Officer Laddy. Bates had worked all night to do a rewrite of the play, which already had only a fraction of the roles in the original work.

"She's such a baby," Perdita said with a sniff, apparently referring to Viola. "You might not know this, but she's actually older than me. She doesn't have much time to make it big. The clock is ticking."

Faith kept her mouth shut, not wanting to fan the flames of rivalry before the performance. But secretly she was thinking that Perdita herself could stand to grow up. She inserted a final hairpin and gave the updo a pat. "There you are. Lovely."

Perdita took hold of Faith's wrist. "Do you really think so?" She peered into the mirror. "People say I resemble my mother."

"Then she must have been a beauty," Faith said gallantly. Perdita was truly a lovely young woman, but all too often, her beauty was overshadowed by her abrasive personality. She stood back to let Perdita out of the chair. "Break a leg tonight."

Minutes later the curtains opened, revealing Leontes's palace.

Sid announced, "Appearing live from Castleton Manor, *The Winter's Tale* by William Shakespeare."

The audience broke into applause, spurred to new heights by the cameras. As for other performances, many in the audience wore period costumes, and the camera made periodic sweeps over them.

The first lines were spoken, and the play began. The bear costume made an appearance. This time it was worn officially, Faith noted with amusement.

After the performance ended, Faith mingled with the guests. Once again the hard-pressed kitchen crew was serving a late supper. This time it featured a variety of baked fowl, including turkey, chicken, duck, and Cornish game hens.

Brooke came up to Faith, adjusting the white baker's cap she wore. "Four down, one to go." She tucked her hands under her apron, watching the servers with an eagle eye.

Faith surveyed her friend, noticing the bluish circles under her eyes. "Did you sleep all right last night?"

"We did. Not a peep from the ghost." Brooke cracked a smile. "Thanks to Watson."

"He came to my rescue again last night." Faith had been so busy, she hadn't had a chance to tell Brooke about the incident with Nell. "Hopefully all the drama is over. That's more tiring than the hard work."

"Agreed." Brooke stiffened, evidently noticing something not to her liking. She darted off, waving. "See you later," she called over her shoulder.

Faith noticed Sid entering the banquet hall, a beautiful woman with dark hair at his side. They stopped every few minutes to greet guests. *That must be his wife*, Faith thought. Noticing Wolfe and Bates standing together, she drifted that way, hoping to join them.

Sid and the woman reached them first, and to Faith's amazement, Bates gave a great cry of surprise. "Beatrice!" he exclaimed, arms wide. "I thought I'd never see you again."

Witnessing their tears and laughter, Faith's first thought was that he must be very good friends with Sid's wife, who looked vaguely familiar. Then the truth hit her, and she gasped. Beatrice was Bates's first wife. Why had she shown up now after all these years?

She quickened her steps to Wolfe's side, arriving in time to hear Beatrice say, "Where is my daughter? I want to congratulate her on such a wonderful performance."

"Daughter?" Bates frowned. "I didn't know you had a child. Or that she was in my troupe."

Beatrice reached up and stroked his cheek. "*We* have a child, darling. Her name is Viola."

Bates swayed on his feet, his complexion going gray, then red. "What? I don't believe it."

Wolfe took his arm. "Come sit down." To the others he said, "This is a bit of a shock, as you can see." Then Wolfe settled the distraught director at the nearest table.

Beatrice joined Bates and rested a hand on his arm. "I'm so sorry. We parted on such bad terms, and you said you never wanted to see me again."

Bates stared at her, his expression heavy with regret. "And you took me at my word." He groaned, putting a hand to his head. "All those years wasted . . . I never saw her grow up. She's so beautiful, so talented." He gazed at Beatrice. "Like her mother."

Beatrice laughed. "The little fiend didn't tell me she had joined your troupe. I was in Venice, minding my own business, when I heard about it. So naturally I got here as soon as I could." She grasped his hand. "Dear Bates, I'm elated to see you again."

Sid made his excuses and faded away.

Very tactful, Faith thought.

"Do you want to go find Viola?" Wolfe asked Faith. "I haven't seen her come in."

"I'd be happy to." Faith headed across the floor toward the hallway. Did Viola know Bates was her father? Or was it all a wonderful coincidence? And how would Perdita react when she found out she had a sister?

It won't be pretty. Faith went first to the dressing rooms. Perhaps Viola was still changing. She'd worn a couple of gowns in the play, but she had said the first one was her favorite and she intended to wear it for the after-party.

But only Eileen was in the dressing room, puttering around with the costumes. "Hello. I'll be out for supper in a few minutes." She placed a gown on a hanger. "I enjoy doing this work, even the tidying up."

"I'm glad—and feeling guilty I wasn't here to help," Faith said. "But tell me, have you seen Viola? You'll never believe it, but her mother is here."

"Her mother? Oh, that is sweet." Eileen shook her head. "I haven't seen Viola since the curtain call. She took off with Griffith."

"Thanks, Eileen." Not pausing to fill her in on Viola's parentage, Faith left the room. She would try calling the actor's suite. She really didn't want a repeat of the other night when she'd barged in on the couple.

At the lobby desk, Faith used the house phone to call the suite.

It rang several times, and then Griffith answered. "Viola? Where have you been?" His voice was eager, almost boyish.

Feeling chagrined at dashing his hopes, Faith said, "I'm sorry, but this is Faith. I'm trying to find Viola. Bates wants to see her." It wasn't up to her to drop the bomb that his girlfriend's mother was at the manor. And that Bates was her father.

Griffith sighed. "Well, she's not here. Or in her room. Tell her I'm looking for her, okay?"

After Faith hung up, she asked the desk clerk for Viola's room number. She dialed it and got no answer.

Faith supposed she'd better do a circuit of the downstairs. She returned to the banquet hall to make sure Viola hadn't shown up there. Then she popped her head into various rooms downstairs. No sign of Viola. None of the staff she encountered had seen the actress either.

Now she'd go up and check Viola's room in person. Maybe she was asleep, which seemed unlikely, or ill, which would be horrible.

At least we don't have to worry about a killer. The judge had refused bail, so Corin was safely locked up.

Faith was tired, and she took the elevator for a change. To her surprise, Marlene was inside when it arrived.

"Heading upstairs already?" Marlene's sharp nose twitched with disapproval. "Viola's mother has arrived, and we need you on-site."

Faith held the door open. "Actually, I'm on my way to Viola's room. She's not down here anywhere."

Patting her omnipresent ring of keys, Marlene stepped back inside the elevator. "Let's go find her."

On the second floor, Marlene led the way to Viola's suite. Marlene knocked, calling, "Miss Grey? Are you there?"

No answer.

Marlene knocked again with the same result.

The keys jingled as she selected the right master. With a twist of the handle, they were in.

When Marlene switched on the light, Faith was startled at the state of the room. A chair lay on its side, and other items were scattered on the carpet. As she shuffled forward, her foot hit a black glove.

She picked it up. It was familiar. Where had she seen it before?

She gasped when she recognized it. The glove was the type Perdita wore when sailing.

20

"Does Viola go frostbite sailing?" Faith asked, holding the glove up for Marlene to see. If so, she had never mentioned it. How odd.

On her way to check the bathroom, Marlene sniffed. "I have no idea. But it looks like Viola isn't here. And what a mess she's made."

"Knock, knock." Griffith entered the room. He glanced around. "Is Viola here?"

"It appears not," Faith said. She showed him the glove. "Is this hers?"

He picked it up with two fingers, distaste in his expression. "No. She hates the cold."

Everything came together in Faith's mind, one puzzle piece fitting neatly with another—or so she hoped. "Does Viola know who her father is?"

Griffith reared back on his heels. "What's that got to do with anything?"

Marlene popped out of the bathroom. "You know what I think about gossip, Faith."

"In this case, it's not gossip." Faith regarded Griffith steadily. "I'll explain in a minute."

Still clutching the glove, Griffith ran his other hand through his rumpled locks. "No, she doesn't. Her mother would never tell her." He grimaced. "It's a very painful topic for her."

"I'm sure," Faith said. "Well, I wasn't going to tell you this, but Bates Beaumont is her father. His ex-wife is here, and she wants to see Viola."

Griffith's face paled. "Bates is her father? Her mother's in Venice—"

"Not anymore. She showed up tonight," Marlene said. "But I didn't know she was married to Bates." Her eyes narrowed, as if accusing Faith of keeping things from her.

"Neither did I until a few minutes ago." Faith plucked the glove out of Griffith's hand and waved it like a flag. "I think Viola is off with Perdita. And knowing that young woman's state of mind, I don't think they're having a good time."

Fortunately, it didn't take much to convince Griffith that something was awry, especially when they found Viola's cell phone under the bed. Rather than go down and try to talk to her parents in public, Faith called Wolfe.

"I think we've got a possible kidnapping situation," she said.

"Again?" he asked.

"I'm afraid so. We're in Viola's room. Can you please bring her parents up here?"

Within a few minutes, Wolfe and the others arrived.

"Where is my baby?" Beatrice asked, wringing her hands.

Bates put an arm around her. "Come sit down, dear. Faith and Wolfe will fill us in."

"Yes, Faith," Wolfe said. "Why don't you start?" He held up his phone. "I'm going to make a call." He stepped out into the hall.

Faith laid out the situation as best she could. "I think Perdita got wind of the fact that Viola is her sister. I believe they're off somewhere together." She didn't want to alarm Viola's mother too much yet. What if the young women were merely in town at a restaurant or pub, getting to know each other as sisters?

She shrugged off the intuition that told her the situation wasn't so innocent. "I gather that Viola didn't know Bates was her father. Or that you were arriving tonight, Ms. Grey?"

Beatrice's face was dead white under her makeup. "Yes on both counts. I didn't know I was pregnant when Bates and I parted, and after Viola was born, it seemed simpler to leave him out of her life. We lived in Europe, and I couldn't bear to send her back here." Blinking away tears, she patted the director's knee. "I'm terribly sorry. It was selfish of me."

Bates took her hand. "We can talk about that later. The issue now is getting her back safely. Perdita is . . . not exactly stable. Her first reaction upon learning she has a sister may not have been one of joy."

Beatrice inhaled sharply, two spots of color appearing on her cheeks. "You mean Viola might be in *danger*?"

Wolfe entered the room. "Unfortunately, that sounds very likely. According to Glenn, our dockmaster, Perdita took her sailboat out tonight. And she wasn't alone."

"Thanks for coming with me," Wolfe said. He held the flashlight steady on the snowy path. "It's unfortunate the coast guard had a shipwreck to attend to."

"No problem." Faith waddled as fast as she could through the freshly fallen snow. She was wearing boots, long johns, wool pants and sweater, and a top layer of insulated windproof clothing. She turned her face up to the overcast sky, feeling flakes touch her face. "I just hope the weather doesn't get any worse."

Wolfe's chuckle was grim. "Me too. The only good news is, the winds aren't too heavy. That means Perdita can't go far and the seas won't swamp her boat."

Faith studied the bay, a pale-gray sheet stretching into the distance. How were they ever going to find Perdita? Their only advantage was Wolfe's knowledge and experience in these waters. And they would be using a motorized boat, which might well be able to overtake the sailboat.

The dockmaster was waiting for them on the dock, his face hidden by a thick woolen hat. "She's all gassed up and ready to go," Glenn said. "Including the emergency kit. The kitchen ran down some provisions too."

Wolfe clapped his employee on the shoulder. "Thanks. Keep the radio on, okay? I'm hoping the coast guard will be able to step in quickly and help."

"I'll do that. I'm sorry I didn't stop them. But Miss Perdita knows her way around a boat. I had no idea—"

"None of us did," Wolfe said. "You can't blame yourself. Let's focus on bringing these young women home."

"Yes sir." Glenn saluted, then helped Faith into the boat tied at the dock. The sleek craft had a glass-enclosed cockpit, especially welcome this time of year.

Wolfe checked the gauges and equipment, then turned the key. The engines began a throaty, powerful rumble that shook Faith's feet. He tuned the radio to a marine frequency.

"Where are we going?" Faith asked as they pulled away from the dock. The boat's powerful lights lit a path across the choppy water.

"Glenn told me Perdita's usual route. It circles out around a couple of small islands. I'm trying that first."

The trip across the empty bay seemed interminable. Urgency beat a rhythm in Faith's midsection. Would they find Perdita and Viola before something tragic occurred? Perdita's impulsive act had taken her down a dangerous path. Running off with her sister wasn't something people would—or should—overlook.

The first island loomed out of the dark, a haunting black shape.

Wolfe slowed, careful to navigate the rocks lining its shores. They made a circuit.

There was no sign of a small white sailboat.

"One down," he said, gunning the motor as he set a fresh course.

The radio, which had crackled now and then with communications from other boats, burst into life. "Mayday! Mayday! Mayday!" a woman screamed.

Wolfe reached over and cranked up the volume.

"Should we respond?" Faith asked.

He shook his head. "I don't want them to know someone's coming. It might change what they do."

"This is the *Tempest*." She repeated the information and added latitude and longitude, then said, "We have struck rocks. Repeat, *Tempest* has struck rocks and needs immediate assistance. There are two women on board, over."

"At least Perdita knows protocol," Wolfe said. "Let's go. They're in trouble."

"Do you know where they are?" Faith asked. The coordinates meant nothing to her.

"Yes, they're on or near Tower Island. I know it well." Wolfe picked up the radio again and gave the coast guard an update. "They'll send someone as soon as they can."

Faith leaned forward in her seat as they sped toward the island. She pictured the small boat slipping into frigid waters. In this weather, the ocean temperatures meant hypothermia, although Perdita's gear extended the length of time someone could safely stay in the water. But what about Viola? Was she prepared for the frigid conditions?

Once again, Wolfe slowed as they approached the landmass, where the water was shallower.

Two arms of rock reached out into the water, and it was upon one of them that Faith spotted the *Tempest*. The small craft lay on its side, heeled over, the mast touching shore and the sails sagging into the water.

"I'm going to get as close as I dare," Wolfe said. "I need you to operate the spotlight for me." He demonstrated how the powerful light worked.

While Wolfe kept the boat in place through careful manipulation of the controls, fighting the tide that pushed toward the rocks, Faith trained the light on the sailboat.

She couldn't see anyone on board.

"They must have made it to shore." Wolfe lifted his chin and inhaled deeply. "Do you smell that?"

Faith sniffed. "Is that smoke?"

"Someone made a fire." Wolfe pointed. "In the tower, no doubt."

She swung the light around, and the beam picked out a stone structure at the peak of the small island. To her relief, lowering the light revealed two sets of prints in the snow. "They're both still alive."

Wolfe nudged the boat into a sandy area, where it was safe to land. "Let's gather emergency supplies and go."

Faith followed Wolfe through the snow, carrying a pack holding heat-reflective blankets and warmers on her shoulders. He was toting water, hot coffee in a thermos, a first aid kit, and food.

The women's footprints made it much easier to walk through the knee-deep snow, which had obviously remained untouched until that evening. The smell of smoke grew stronger the closer they got, and Faith saw a stream of smoke drifting out of the upper window. She also heard screams.

Wolfe began to run, his long legs closing up the distance.

Faith valiantly tried to move faster, but she floundered in the drifts. Finally, she reached the tower, where a huge wooden door stood open.

Wolfe paused at the foot of a spiral staircase winding around to the second story. He put a finger to his lips, then gently set his pack on the floor. His gesture instructed her to do the same.

Slowly, oh so slowly, Wolfe crept up the stairs.

She followed a couple of steps below, careful not to let her boots scrape on the stone.

The yelling continued, mostly Perdita by the sounds of it, although Faith also discerned Viola's lighter voice.

The tower room was lit only by anemic flames in the fireplace. Perdita was breaking sticks over her knee to feed the flames. No doubt the wood was wet, hence the poor burning and smoke.

Viola sat opposite the doorway. Her eyes widened when she noticed Wolfe and Faith.

He put a finger to his lips to warn her to be quiet.

Perdita rose from her crouch. "You know, *Sister*, there's room for only one of us in our father's life. He never cared a bit about you, so why are you trying to horn in now?"

Viola bit her lip. "I'm not. *You* said that. I didn't even know until tonight that he was my father."

Her sister advanced on her, making Viola cower back against the wall. "I don't believe you. You got this gig on purpose. To take my place." The much taller woman loomed over the tiny actress. "Only one of us is leaving this tower."

Faith and Wolfe stared at each other. This was getting far too serious.

"You're going to kill me?" Viola shrieked. "Why? I never did anything to you."

"Except be born. First." Perdita's voice dropped to a menacing whisper. "So the *Folio* will be yours."

The *First Folio* that was worth millions of dollars. How much did that valuable book play into Perdita's plan to get rid of her perceived rival?

"I don't want the *Folio*," Viola shot back. "I don't care about it."

"Right. Why would you? Famous and beautiful as you are. But it's all I have." Perdita stood straight and began to pace.

While her back was turned, Viola shrugged, as though asking what to do.

Wolfe made a staying gesture, then mouthed, "Warn her."

Viola screamed and pointed a shaking finger. "I think someone's coming."

Perdita snorted. "What are you talking about? No one is going to be here for hours. The coast guard is busy with a shipwreck."

"No, I heard something. Footsteps," Viola said, injecting fear into her voice.

"Right." Perdita marched across the floor. She shoved the door all the way open and leaned out to view the staircase.

Wolfe grabbed her and yanked her down. He pulled out a rope

from his jacket pocket and managed to tie it on one of the woman's thrashing arms.

Perdita screamed and fought.

Leaving him to it, Faith darted past and entered the tower room. "Viola, are you all right?"

"Oh, I'm so glad to see you." Viola rose, bracing a hand on a window ledge, and gave Faith a big hug. "I'm okay. Kind of cold." She wore winter clothing, but the pants were soaked up to the knees.

"We brought blankets and a thermos of coffee," Faith said. "Wait here, and I'll go get them."

Wolfe entered the room. "I lost her."

Faith's heart lurched. "She can't take our boat, can she?"

"No, I have the key." Wolfe held it up. "Besides, she ran in the opposite direction."

Faith glanced out the closest window. A dark figure flailed through the snow, headed toward a white expanse surrounded by small trees. "Where's she going?"

Wolfe joined her at the window. "To the pond." He gave a yelp. "The ice won't hold her. Stay here, you two. I'm going after her." He ran out the door.

The pair watched as Perdita reached the pond and began to cross it.

The ice gave way, and Perdita disappeared with a scream.

The sky was lightening toward dawn when Wolfe guided the boat to dock at Castleton Manor.

"We made it," Faith said, exultant.

Perdita and Viola were aboard the coast guard cutter, the first under guard and the second staying nice and warm after being checked over for injury.

The officials had shown up right after Wolfe hauled Perdita from the frosty pond. The rope on her wrist had caught on a branch, preventing her from going underwater and drowning.

Faith believed the young woman was suffering from a breakdown. She'd most likely be admitted to a hospital for treatment. Despite being terrified by her sister's erratic behavior, Viola had expressed concern for her well-being.

Glenn came out to the dock to tie up the boat. "Welcome back, Mr. Jaxon and Miss Newberry."

"Good to be here," Wolfe said. "Home sweet home at last." He turned to Faith. "Hot drinks and a fire are waiting for us in my apartment."

She nodded. She'd heard him make the call. But she doubted she'd ever feel truly warm again. The cold had seeped into her very bones, and her heart felt like a block of ice after watching Perdita threaten her sister's life.

When they entered the Jaxon apartment living room, a small group rose to greet them.

Watson mewed and sprinted toward his person.

Faith gathered him into her arms, tears springing to her eyes. He purred loudly and rubbed his face against her chin.

Charlotte clapped. "What a magnificent creature."

"He certainly is." Eileen hugged Faith, followed by Brooke and Laura.

Marlene merely smiled as she served Faith and Wolfe steaming cups of hot chocolate.

Seated close to the roaring fire, with Watson on her lap and a hot drink in her hand, Faith thought she might thaw out eventually after all.

"What happened on the island?" Charlotte asked, seated next to Wolfe on a sofa.

Wolfe took them through the bizarre series of events. "Bates and Beatrice are with Viola and Perdita right now," he concluded. "And the police will be taking full statements tomorrow." He glanced at the mantel clock. "I mean, today."

"How in the world did Perdita find out about Viola?" Eileen asked. "Her own father didn't know she existed."

Faith had wondered that very thing.

"Viola told us that Perdita became obsessed with Beatrice after her own mother died," Wolfe replied. "She'd studied everything she could find about her. Then she realized a photograph of Viola onstage was very similar to one of Beatrice in the same role. So Perdita hired a private detective. He managed to track Beatrice down in Italy and learned she and Bates had a daughter. It wasn't long before he discovered who that daughter was."

"Jealousy can be a terrible thing," Charlotte said.

Others murmured agreement.

"The man Perdita met with here was the private detective," Wolfe continued. "He was delivering the dossier on Viola."

"So Perdita wasn't trying to sell the *First Folio*," Faith said.

"The *Folio* was in Perdita's room, just as Mr. Beaumont believed," Marlene answered. Her expression was decidedly sour.

Faith remembered that Wolfe had loaned Bates the keys to the library and the case where the *First Folio* had been displayed. Then she thought of something else. "Perdita must have been getting into the library after hours. I found cat treats all over the floor."

"Oh, Perdita was a sneaky one," Marlene said. "And we found out that Nell sweet-talked the cleaner into letting her go into your room, Faith. One of her 'pranks.'" She put air quotes around the last word.

"Corin had the garage key from when he was here as a teen," Wolfe said, then turned to his mother. "I think it's time to change the locks all around."

Obviously alarmed, Marlene put a hand to her waist, although she wasn't wearing her famous ring of keys at the moment.

Charlotte frowned. "Go ahead. But I don't want those electronic things. They'll spoil the atmosphere."

Marlene visibly relaxed when Wolfe agreed.

Someone knocked on the doorjamb, and they turned to see Officer Laddy. He shifted uncomfortably under their collective gaze. "The door was open . . ." His voice trailed off.

"Please come in," Wolfe said. "Help yourself to hot chocolate on the table."

"Thanks, but I'm not here to stay. I just wanted to let you know that the chief wants to do the statements at noon." The officer squirmed, an uneasy look on his features. "But I have a favor to ask."

"What is it?" Wolfe asked kindly.

Officer Laddy appeared to be bracing himself. "Will you coach me on my lines for *Romeo and Juliet*? I'd hate to make a fool of myself and ruin the production."

Wolfe laughed. "Of course." He gestured to Faith with a smile. "After Faith finishes coaching me."

"Whatever works," Charlotte said. She sighed. "I never thought I'd say this, but I'll be glad when the event is over."

"In this case, parting will *not* be sweet sorrow," Wolfe quipped.

Watson meowed as if in agreement, and everyone laughed.

YOUR FEEDBACK MEANS A LOT TO US!

Up to this point, we've been doing all the writing. Now it's *your* turn!

Tell us what you think about this book, the characters, the bad guy, or anything else you'd like to share with us about this series. We can't wait to hear from *you*!

Log on to give us your feedback at:
https://www.surveymonkey.com/r/CastletonLibrary

Annie's FICTION

Learn more about Annie's fiction books at

AnniesFiction.com

We've designed the Annie's Fiction website especially for you!

Access your e-books and audiobooks • Manage your account

Choose from one of these great series:

Amish Inn Mysteries	Chocolate Shoppe Mysteries
Annie's Attic Mysteries	Creative Woman Mysteries
Annie's Mysteries Unraveled	Hearts of Amish Country
Annie's Quilted Mysteries	Inn at Magnolia Harbor
Annie's Secrets of the Quilt	Secrets of the Castleton Manor Library
Annie's Sweet Intrigue	Scottish Bakehouse Mysteries
Antique Shop Mysteries	Victorian Mansion Flower Shop Mysteries

What are you waiting for? Visit us now at **AnniesFiction.com!**